The Lying Voices

Elizabeth Ferrars

NEW ENGLISH LIBRARY
Hodder and Stoughton

Copyright © 1954 M. D. Brown

First published in Great Britain in 1954
by William Collins Sons & Co Ltd

First published in paperback in 1996
by Hodder and Stoughton
A division of Hodder Headline PLC

An NEL paperback

The right of Elizabeth Ferrars to be identified as the Author of
the Work has been asserted by her in accordance with the
Copyright, Designs and Patents Act 1988.

10 9 8 7 6 5 4 3 2 1

A CIP catalogue record for this title is available from the British Library

ISBN 0 340 64055 3

Printed and bound in Great Britain by
Cox & Wyman Ltd, Reading, Berkshire

Hodder and Stoughton
A division of Hodder Headline PLC
338 Euston Road
London NW1 3BH

When he arrived in Archersfield and got off the bus, he remembered that he had still no shillings for the meter in his room and that he had not yet bought a Sunday paper. Not very hopeful that the newsagent would still be open, he started across the square towards the shop.

Again something stopped him before he reached it.

Someone was standing in the doorway of the shop, barring his entrance. It was a girl, who was reading a newspaper. She was holding the paper opened out before her and was staring at some paragraph in it with a look of horrified amazement on her face. The coat she was wearing was of bright scarlet.

I

FROM EARLY in the morning until late in the evening of the day on which Arnold Thaine was murdered, the rain fell.

It fell steadily and quietly. There was no wind to drive it aslant and no perceptible motion of cloud across the low and level sky.

This gave a kind of peacefulness to the streaming daylight and the pattering dusk. Other sounds died in the swish of the raindrops falling through the trees. Distances were blotted out of sight. Windows were closed against the long downpour. No one who could escape it walked the wet roads or the swamped field-paths.

Only for a few minutes, during the morning, almost mysteriously, the sun shone. A narrow streak of blue appeared in the grey overhead and a rainbow arched itself suddenly above the puddled fields. But as soon as it was possible to be certain that this had happened, it was over. The brightness vanished and the rain came as before and did not cease until some late hour of darkness. Long before that time, Arnold Thaine had been murdered.

In the room where his body lay, undiscovered for several hours, no one could have told when the rain stopped, for the room contained at least a hundred clocks, and their ticking, not unlike a crazily amplified echo of the rain itself, swallowed the sound of it, as the rain had swallowed other smaller sounds.

The clocks ticked in a hundred different rhythms, loudly or softly, on high or low notes, some striking the hours sweetly and some with a jangle and some letting them pass without comment of any kind. But one thing all the clocks had in common. Every single one in that room, big or little, shabby or splendid, grotesque or beautiful, was wrong.

During the few minutes of sunshine in the morning,

Justin Emery, coming out of his hotel into the market square of Archersfield, saw a girl in a scarlet coat descend from a bus.

But for the sunshine falling on the brave red coat and on her bright, fair hair, he might not have noticed her, for he was hurrying to catch the bus before it started again. However, for a moment, as she reached the pavement, she stood in his way, facing him, and he received a vivid impression, that he later remembered clearly, of her sunlit youth and beauty.

Looking uncertainly around her, she began to cross the square. A dog that had been sniffing along the gutter looked up as she approached and started to wag his tail. He was an ugly, surly-looking mongrel and the tail was only a stump, but he seemed to share in the feeling that Justin Emery took on to the bus with him, that the girl and the moment of sunshine were somehow connected and that, as she walked off in the direction of the Norman church, that she had probably come to Archersfield to see, she was carrying some of the gleam away with her, as if it were a private possession.

By the time that the bus moved on from the square, the big raindrops were once more splashing into puddles which for those few minutes had shone with light, but now again looked dull and slimy.

Justin asked the conductor to tell him when the bus reached Fallow Corner, then settled down in a seat at the rear and lit a cigarette. As he did so, he became aware that an uneasiness and slight depression had returned. It had been on his mind, except for those few minutes when the sun had so unexpectedly shone, ever since the evening before, when he had spoken to Grace DeLong on the telephone.

It was only a vague feeling, this depression, a faint sense of discomfort. But it drew his brows into an unconscious frown and brought a guarded look into his large, intent eyes. The fault, he had been telling himself, had really been his own. Having been so incautious as to re-enter Grace DeLong's life abruptly by telephone, after an absence of six years, he had had no right to expect any great warmth in his reception.

Yet that memory of the muteness of the instrument at his ear after he had told her his name, still worried him. Even the fact that after some minutes of hesitant conversation, she had invited him to lunch the next day and then had insisted on his coming early, because, of course, they would have so much to tell one another, had not removed the chill that had been caused by her having had nothing at all to say at the sound of his name.

The rain covered the window beside him with a sheet of water. Through it he saw small, grey stone houses and after them flat fields. The autumnal hedges had been almost stripped of their leaves, except for an occasional hollybush, with its berries reddening.

Berries plentiful and early, he remembered, were supposed to promise a cold winter. For a moment the thought pleased him. It was six years since he had experienced a real winter and he looked forward to it.

But then the thought followed that when the time came he might no longer be here. This was a thought typical of him at present, that went with a habit he had of acting with a sudden impulsiveness which took the place of the power to make real decisions. Anything, he felt, might happen to him at any time. It was not in him to cause it or prevent it. But though he had sometimes been envied for the ease with which he uprooted himself, changing the whole course of his life, apparently, after a few minutes' thought, the truth was that in the moment of sudden action he was nearly always beset by an intense reluctance to act at all, of longing for the strength to hold back, to take no part in what was about to happen.

" Fallow Corner ! " Far sooner than he had been expecting it, the voice of the conductor reached him, and the bus came to a stop under some dripping trees. Justin got up and jumped down into the road.

As the bus moved on again, he saw, in the hedge on the other side of the road, the blue gate that Grace had described to him and beyond it the house that she had described. It

was a grey stone house with a blue door outlined in pale
yellow and with pale yellow window-frames. Such colouring
alone would have identified the house as hers, without her
description.

Walking up the flagged path, bordered on both sides with
cropped lavender bushes, Justin rang the bell. He was
annoyed, but for some reason not genuinely surprised, when
no one answered.

He stood hesitating. A small porch sheltered him from
the rain, but it was cold. Driving his fists down deep into
his pockets and hunching his shoulders, he stood listening
for the sound of movement within the house.

He was a more forbidding figure, as he stood there, than
he himself was aware. The loose raincoat made him look
broader than he was and the lowered hat-brim, hiding the
high forehead, from which the greying hair had receded, cast
a shadow over the rather anxious brown eyes. His annoyance creased sharp wrinkles in his rather fleshy cheeks and
gave his face a cadaverousness that was not natural to it.
The damp cold made it pale.

As he stood there, uncertain what to do next, it came to
him all at once how familiar this experience had recently
become, this standing before a closed door, waiting. Again
and again, during the last few weeks, doors had not opened,
telephones had not been answered, or, if they had been,
only strange faces and strange voices had greeted him.

And what could one ever do with a closed door but walk
away from it?

"Justin!"

A car door had slammed in the road.

Talking breathlessly, Grace DeLong, in a tweed suit that
Justin was sure she had possessed six years before, came
hurrying up the path from the blue gate.

"I saw the bus, I knew you must have got here, I was so
afraid you wouldn't have waited. But I simply couldn't help
it. I had to go to the Thaines."

She held out both her hands to him.

He brought his out of his pockets to grasp them. Hers
were small, hard hands. Like his, they were cold.

" I'm so glad you thought of coming," she said, still talking gaspingly, as if she had been running, instead of driving a car. " It's one of the nicest things that's happened for ages. I thought you'd gone for ever. But for ever ! "

Her small, puppyish face smiled up at him, though her short-sighted eyes did not quite succeed in focusing on his. For a moment he thought that she was going to kiss him. But then she drew her hands out of his and grasped the door handle. The blue door swung open.

" It wasn't locked," she said. " You should have gone straight in."

" I didn't know it wasn't locked," he answered.

" We never lock things here," she said, as if he ought to have known that without being told.

Following her as she went inside, he felt as helplessly mute as she had been the evening before on the telephone. Yet she had not changed much, or so he thought at first. Her short, dark hair, swinging loosely as she tossed it back from her face in a rather consciously childish gesture, was hardly greyer than when he had seen her last. Her face had no more wrinkles than he had been prepared to find there. She moved with the same vigour as ever, in the same hurrying, uneven way, and in general the slight signs of the loss of youth had made little difference to her.

However, when she looked him up and down and said, " You've changed, you know—you've changed a great deal. You look as if things had been happening to you," she was putting into words something that had been forming in his mind concerning her.

She went on : " I'd hoped you wouldn't have changed. I'd hoped we'd be able to pick up the past just as it was. That's what we've always been able to do before. That's to say—well, I don't know. But I don't seem to have the energy for new things now."

Still at a loss what to say, he saw that she was waiting for him to reply.

" Who are these Thaines you mentioned ? " he asked. " Aren't they new ? "

" Arnold Thaine," she said, as if that explained everything.

The name did evoke a faint feeling of familiarity. It was one that Justin thought that he ought to know. But Grace had always had a trick of making her acquaintances sound like people with whose names everyone should be familiar.

" Furniture design," Grace said. " He's done lots of other things too, but it's been furniture now for a good many years. And clocks. But that's just a hobby. Actually, that's the rather crazy, putting-off side of him that I can't . . . Well, I don't know how to describe it, but just imagine a room full of clocks, all going, and a man sitting there in the middle of them to work. But he's wonderful, really, and so's his work. His workshops are near here. I went in one day by accident ; that's how I got to know him and Hester. And I've bought some of his things. I'll show them to you. . . . Only why are we talking about the Thaines when you haven't even started to tell me about yourself and what suddenly gave you the idea of coming all the way down here to see me ? Was it really just to see me, or have you some scheme on hand ? "

" No, I've no scheme," he said. " I just wanted to see you."

She frowned a little, as if she had to puzzle it out.

" Well, come in here," she said, opening a door into a small sitting-room. " We'll have some sherry and you can start telling me about things. But what made you ask me about Arnold ? "

" I don't know," he said. Though he had never been in the room before, it seemed familiar, for it had the same furniture in it, the modern paintings and the same rather bizarre kind of colouring, that he remembered in her house in London. " It was just that I didn't know what else to say. I hadn't thought of its being difficult to pick up the threads, but it is, so I said the only thing that came into my head."

" Yes," she said, " it's difficult, of course it is. There's too much to say and we're both choked with it all. All the same, what made you mention the Thaines ? "

" It was you who mentioned them first," he said. " You said you'd had to go there."

" Oh yes. But that was nothing important. It was just

something I wanted to ask them and as it happened, both of them were out, so I needn't have gone at all. If I'd thought that there'd be any risk of missing you, I shouldn't have gone. But your bus was a bit early, wasn't it ? "

" Quite likely," he said.

In fact, it had been late. The bus should have left the square at ten minutes past eleven, but had actually done so at nearer twenty minutes past the hour.

" I'm sure it was early," Grace said. " It often is. Or terribly late. You never know which it's going to be. Time doesn't mean anything to the people here."

" Except to the man with a roomful of clocks."

" Oh, but it isn't *time* that interests him—all the clocks are wrong. Now which would you prefer, sherry or—no, there's no gin left. I never can keep gin in the house these days, ever since Ben Eagan found out that I've generally got it. You don't know Ben. He works for Arnold. That's to say, he's learning the work from him, and when he's learnt it and developed a bit—he's very young still—he's going to be the more brilliant of the two. Even Arnold himself says so. But why do we keep on talking about those Thaines ? You aren't interested. Come and sit by the fire —are you used to fires yet ?—and tell me all about the queer things you've been doing."

" None of them were very queer," he said.

" Oh, but with you things are always queer. To start life with a First in Philosophy, then get rich in industry, then disappear in Australia. . . . But why did you disappear, Justin ? What was the real reason ? "

They had sat down on either side of a banked-up fire that Grace now jabbed at with the poker, so that flames burst through the black crust of coal dust and flickered up against the back of the chimney.

The warmth of it, together with the sherry, began to drive out the chill of the rain. Stretching out comfortably in the deep chair, Justin said, " I didn't think of it as disappearing. I always meant to write."

" Oh, one always means to write. Only one doesn't really. Isn't that the truth ? "

" I'm not sure that it is. It's just that writing's a bore. There were plenty of times when I wanted to see you."

" Wasn't there anyone else you did write to ? "

" My sisters, occasionally."

" Didn't you write to Marion Garston ? "

" I don't think I did."

" Wasn't she the real reason why you disappeared, Justin ? "

The question annoyed him, but more, he believed, because it was almost difficult to remember the answer than for any other reason.

" Partly, perhaps," he said. " I suppose that situation had got beyond me. But really I just suddenly decided, when I got to Sydney on that business trip that was supposed to last a month, that I'd like to stay on. It was all so different. And suddenly I had an opportunity offered me to go into business with a man—a new sort of business."

" What was it ? "

" Running a hotel."

" You ! "

" Why not ? "

" But why have you come home then ? "

" We sold out last summer."

" At a loss ? "

" Oh no, at a profit, a good profit."

Grace threw back her head, laughing. The short, dark hair swung childishly about her face.

" Philosophy must be a wonderful training for life. You're richer than ever now, I suppose."

" I never was rich," he said.

It was Grace who had always been rich. First she had had wealth inherited from her parents, then more had come to her when her husband had died, one year after their marriage.

But she had always chosen, for some unexplained reason, to mock Justin because he had turned out to be capable of earning good salaries in slightly unexpected kinds of job. She had always seemed to find this very funny and perhaps a little bit shocking.

" I suppose you know Marion's married again," she went on.

" No, I don't know anything," he said.

" I believe that marriage too is a flop," Grace said. " That's what I've been told. But I don't see her nowadays. She never liked me, except just at first, before she'd met you. She was always madly jealous, even when there was no reason to be. I dare say that's why the marriages go wrong."

He thought of telling her then how dim the image of Marion had become, and how little shock there had been to him in her information. However, instead, he said, " Talking of disappearing, who'd have believed, when you disappeared down here in the war, that you'd have stayed on so long ? I thought that the day the peace was signed, you'd have been back in London."

" Why should I go back to London ? " she asked.

" Well, with the children at school, aren't you alone a great deal ? "

" I rather like being alone. Besides . . ." She paused, then appeared to forget to go on with her sentence.

Besides, Justin concluded it for her in his mind, she wasn't alone. There were the Thaines. There was the brilliant young man who drank her gin. Probably it was all much as it had been in London.

" I like being alone," she repeated after a moment, with a curious aggressiveness in her tone, as if she were prepared to argue with him about it. " I don't even have servants now. I hate the feeling of people around me all the time. I just have a woman in to clean once a week. So in a minute or two you'll have to excuse me while I go and get the lunch. Or you can come and talk to me in the kitchen, if you like. Perhaps you'd better do that, because quite soon after lunch I've got to go out and I shan't have seen half enough of you by then. By the way, how long are you staying in Archersfield ? "

It brought him up short. He had hardly considered how long he intended to stay, but he had not expected to be dismissed by Grace immediately after lunch.

To make matters worse now, she entered on a long, hurried and muddled description of all the things that she was compelled to do that afternoon. None of them sounded so important to Justin that a call on the telephone might not have delayed them. But for some reason he did not suggest that such a call should be made. Annoyance at himself for the impulse that had brought him here to receive such offhand treatment made him look bored and absent-minded. The worst of it was that he had half-expected it. Grace had always been like that.

She seemed to sense the effect that her rambling explanations were having upon him, for suddenly breaking them off, she leant towards him and fixing her ill-focused eyes on his face, asked again, more insistently, "How long are you staying in Archersfield, Justin?"

"I was thinking of catching the evening train," he said, though he was not even certain that there was one.

"What, to-day?"

"Yes."

"Oh no! No, you mustn't do that. Stay at least until to-morrow. Or the day after. But at least until to-morrow. Please."

She stretched out a hand to him.

Instead of being pleased by it, Justin was disturbed. The possibility that he might really intend to leave that evening seemed to have startled some sharp anxiety in her. He realised then that he had sensed this anxiety working in her ever since she had come hurrying breathlessly up the garden path towards him.

Feeling some uncertainty in him, she went on rapidly, "I'll call for you to-morrow morning with the car and we'll go and see the Thaines. I'll get Arnold to show you the workshops. You'll really find that worth while. He's got some beautiful things in hand and it's always fascinating to hear a real craftsman talking about his work. Then we'll get him and Hester and Ben too to come to the local with us. You'll enjoy that. And afterwards . . ." She paused. Then she added in a low tone, "You will stay at least till to-morrow, won't you?"

" Well," he said, " I suppose I——"

She jumped up. " Good. Now I'll go and get lunch and you can help yourself to some more sherry, then come along to the kitchen and talk to me while I cook. Not that I'm clever enough to talk lucidly when I'm trying to cook. It seems to take all my attention. It's such a nuisance, isn't it, having so little time to-day ? But to-morrow it'll be different. We'll have lots of time to talk to-morrow."

She hurried out.

Justin finished the sherry in his glass, refilled it from the decanter on the table. But then he lingered in the sitting-room, not really much attracted by the thought of that talk in the kitchen.

To-morrow, as Grace had said, they would have lots of time for talking. They would have lots of time for talking in the presence of other people, which might, after all, be the best way for him and Grace to talk at present.

Was she in love with this man Thaine, he wondered. Was that the trouble ?

Then he told himself that perhaps there was no trouble at all, except the six years of unshared experience and the unalterable fact that Grace was a very irritating woman.

In that Justin was mistaken.

Grace DeLong was in great trouble, as one glance at her white, rain-streaked face told him, when, late that same evening, she came suddenly into the hotel lounge, where Justin, with a last drink, was sitting alone by the fire, about to go up to bed.

As soon as she saw him, her eyes brimmed over with tears. Hurrying across the room to him with her quick, uneven stride, she caught hold of his arm with both hands. By their tense grasp he could feel that her whole body was trembling.

" Thank God you're here," she said, then she choked and could not go on. But with her small, strong hands on his arm, she started pulling him towards the door.

" What is it ?—Grace, stop ! " he said. " What's happened ? "

" It's Arnold."

" What's happened ? "

" He's dead. He's been murdered. Oh, come along quickly, Justin. Don't wait. We must go there at once. All along, this is what I've been afraid of. And I was there . . ."

This time he did not resist her when she caught his arm. Together they went out into the darkness and the rain that still came pouring steadily down, as it had all day, hissing on the wet pavements, flooding the gutters and filling the night with a hasty, pattering sound, as of hundreds of clocks ticking.

II

GRACE'S SMALL car was parked in the square.

Taking the road back to Fallow Corner, she sat slumped forward over the wheel, her eyes narrowed as she peered through the rainwashed windscreen. Her profile in the darkness, had a hard, resolute outline. But her voice was shaking as, in a gasping, hysterical tone, she cried, " Damn, oh damn, I ought to have brought my glasses ! I can't see to drive properly without my glasses ! "

She swung the wheel sharply and the car shot out of the square. Its tyres jolted against the kerb and sent a wave of muddy water from the gutter washing over the pavement.

A passer-by tried to escape the wave, then stood still, shouting after them.

" Shall I drive ? " Justin asked.

" No, I'll manage," Grace answered curtly.

Justin saw the car-lights sweep over the same small, stone houses that he had seen that morning from the bus. But when the houses came to an end, hedges that looked very tall, seen from the low car, shut out his view of the fields.

" Now," he said a minute or two later, " suppose we stop and talk a bit."

" We can't stop," she said.

" Why not ? "

" I want to get there."

Yet after a moment she stopped the car, and folding her arms on the wheel, buried her face in them.

Justin felt for his cigarettes. When Grace heard the scrape of the match, she raised her head, held out her hand and said, " Give me one."

He gave her a cigarette and lit it for her. She drew the smoke in deeply, choked over it and coughed. He let her get over it, though his nerves were tingling with her panic and his impulse was to shout at her or shake her.

After a moment she said, half-angrily, " You're so calm."

" Not me. You've got me scared almost out of my wits," he said.

" You've nothing to be scared of."

" Well, when you say things like murder. . . . You did say murder, didn't you ? I'm not imagining things ? "

" No." She started coughing again. " That's what I said."

" Well then, go on and tell me about it."

" I hardly know anything—only that it happened."

He put a hand on her shoulder. " Listen, Grace, I'm coming with you if you want me to, but I want to know, before we get there, what we're getting into. So try to talk. Go on, try."

" But I don't know anything, only that Hester rang me up and told me she'd found him and that the police were coming."

" Hester is Thaine's wife ? "

" Yes."

" And it's Thaine who's dead ? "

The tip of her cigarette glowed in the darkness, momentarily lighting up her haggard face. " Yes."

" Did she say it was murder ? " Justin asked. " Did she use the word ? "

" Yes."

" Are you sure ? "

" Of course I'm sure. What are you thinking ? D'you think I'd make up a thing like that ? Good God . . ."

" Wait ! " he begged. " How did she know it was murder ? "

" How should I know ? She hardly said anything—only just that—murder and the police coming."

" Did she ask you to go straight round ? "

" Yes. No. Yes, she did."

" You aren't sure ? "

" I'm not sure of anything she said after she'd said that about murder."

" Then why are you going ? "

Her voice quivered hysterically. " These people are my friends ! We've been seeing each other almost every day for years. We walk into each other's houses as if we belonged there. We meet at the pub. We do things for each other if we get ill. And you, who calmly disappeared for six years and walk in suddenly as if that was of no importance, ask me *why* . . . ! "

" Yes," he said. " But you came and fetched me, remember. Why did you do that ? "

" I just thought . . . I felt . . ." She paused. " I hardly know. Go back if you want to."

" No, I'm going with you. But there are still things I want you to tell me before we go on. Just now in the hotel you said that you'd been expecting this all along. What did you mean ? "

" I never said that."

" You did."

" That's quite untrue. I know just what I said. I told you that Arnold was dead—murdered—and I asked you to come with me. Well, if you don't want to, don't. I don't mind. But I'm afraid that I want to get on to the Thaines as quickly as I can, so I can't take you back to your hotel."

" It's all right, we'll go on," Justin said. " But you did say that you'd been expecting it and also that you were there when it happened and if I knew more about that, I might be able to help you a little more when we get there. As it is, I don't see what use I'm going to be."

She remained crouched over the wheel, staring ahead

through the wet windscreen, the cigarette jutting at an angle from her tight lips.

Justin waited a moment, then asked, " *Were* you there, Grace ? "

She gave a slight shake of her head. But the movement had an almost absent-minded look, as if, all of a sudden, some quite different thought had taken possession of her.

" I wasn't there when it happened," she said quietly. " I didn't say I was. Or I didn't mean it. Of course, if you say I said it, I suppose I did, but I meant something else. And about having expected it, if I said that, it was just hysteria, a sort of . . . Well, I'll explain another time. But I'm glad it was you I said it to. You've known me such a long time. You know what I'm like."

" I still don't understand," he said, " and I'd still like to know what it was you meant when you said that you were there."

Wearily, as if he were intolerably slow of comprehension, she said, " I was there earlier."

" Earlier than the murder ? "

" Of course. That's to say, when I went to the house, I didn't find Arnold or his body. So when Hester told me——"

He interrupted. " Why did you go ? "

" To arrange about to-morrow. You remember, I was going to take you to see the Thaines and I just wanted to make sure that they'd be there."

" Why didn't you simply telephone ? "

A wild note shrilled in her voice again. " What are you trying to do to me, Justin ? Are you trying to show that I had something to do with this murder ? "

Carefully he kept his own voice quiet. " It was raining, wasn't it ? " he said reasonably. " It was raining cats and dogs. Not nice to go out in. Yet you went rushing round there instead of telephoning. Why ? "

"I did telephone," she said. "I telephoned several times. But no one answered. So I thought I'd go round there in case the trouble was that the line was out of order. We've had a good deal of trouble with that lately and I didn't want to risk upsetting our plans for to-morrow. But when I got to the house there was no one in."

" Yet you went straight in ? "

" Yes, I told you we always do that."

" Yes, so you did. But I wish you could think of a better reason for having gone to the house. When the police start asking you questions, you're going to find that answer will sound awfully thin, even in your own ears."

Leaning back, she let her hands fall into her lap, and remained like that, very still. Then she drew a long breath. " There'll be no need for you to mention to anyone what I said to you, will there ? About my having been to the house and about having expected—all this—if I really said that."

" I won't say that you said either thing to me," he said, " but you shouldn't try to keep from the police the fact that you went to the house this afternoon."

" I don't think anyone saw me."

" That's something you can't be sure of. And if anyone did, and you don't mention it yourself, it'll look as if you'd a reason for concealing that visit. And let me say this, too. If you really did expect this to happen——"

" I didn't," she broke in. " It's just that I expected *something* to happen—but not this."

" What sort of thing, then ? "

" I don't know. Anything. Things couldn't have gone on as they were."

There was a silence.

Then Justin asked, " Grace, were you in love with Thaine ? "

" Oh no," she said.

" Is that the truth ? "

" Why, yes." Her tone was almost casual. " I was quite fond of him and I admired him, but in love. . . . No, he wasn't my kind of man at all. Much too dominating and aggressively male—and aware of it too. I've never been attracted by that."

In that last statement at least, Justin knew that there was truth. Beginning with her husband, Dick DeLong, Grace had always been attracted by rather girlish-looking and dependent men, usually younger than herself. But then, what, in her relationship with the Thaines, was she so determined to conceal ? What was she afraid of betraying ?

" What kind of person is Hester Thaine ? " Justin asked.

" I don't know."

" Don't *know* ? But I thought——"

" Oh yes, we're friends. Sort of. But in the country one becomes friends with people simply because they're there. The fact that they may be the sort of people one's congenitally incapable of understanding isn't important."

" You don't really like her, then ? "

" Oh, I do. She's a nice woman, she's intelligent, she's kind. But I've never really grasped what goes on inside her and I never will, so I can't answer your question."

" I see."

" Do you ? Only you don't believe me. I do like Hester. I like her a good deal better than I ever liked Arnold. Still, that doesn't matter. Hester didn't do the murder. She was away in Wallport all day."

" Did she tell you that on the telephone ? "

" I don't remember. But she always goes into Wallport every Saturday, shopping."

" Always ? "

" I think so. There's a market there on Saturdays. Why?"

" Oh, I just want to get as much of the whole picture as I can before I'm involved in it."

He did not point out that Grace had visited the Thaines' house twice that day when apparently she had had reason to believe that Hester Thaine would be absent from it, in Wallport.

" Shall we drive on now ? " he said.

" All right."

The car shot forward.

It was just then that Justin felt, at its most intense, his ever-recurring reluctance to proceed one step further in the direction in which events were carrying him.

He felt only horror at the thought of what lay ahead. To be taken among complete strangers at a moment of terrible crisis in their lives, for no very good reason except that

Grace wanted to cling to him for a kind of support which he knew her well enough to expect she would reject suddenly and without explanations when the mood came to her to do so, struck him as a prospect so detestable that the only thing to be done was somehow to leap out of the car and disappear in the darkness and the rain.

Justin had spent a good deal of that day, after he had returned to his hotel from Fallow Corner, sitting in the lounge, ostensibly reading, but in reality engaged in an argument with himself concerning his motives in seeking Grace out after all this time. What had he expected ? What had he wanted ? Had there been anything more behind his desire to see her than the fact that, although he seldom consciously sentimentalised the past, he was singularly incapable of cutting himself free from it ?

Because, as a girl and the young wife of his friend, Dick DeLong, Grace with her bright, puppyish face, her tossing hair, her quick mind and her great emotional energy, had had a certain importance for Justin, he appeared to feel that he and she still owed something to one another.

In fact, he thought, puzzled at himself and at the discovery, it was almost as if, in coming here, he had expected to pay and to collect a debt. But that was nonsense.

III

" Look, there it is," Grace said. " The Thaines' house."

He saw it ahead of them, a long, low house, its side pierced with lighted windows.

" And those cars, I suppose, mean the police are there," he said.

" Yes—oh hell, look at that ! " Grace braked the car violently as a dog leapt out at them from the hedge, barking wildly. The front wheel of the car, barely missing him, jolted on to the verge.

" Are you sure you want me to come in with you ? " Justin said. " I could wait here for you."

" Of course I want you to come in," she said. " That's why I fetched you. But if you don't want to . . ."

In reply, he opened the door beside him and swung his legs out of the car.

The dog rushed at him, snarling. He was a big, surly-looking mongrel with small ears laid wickedly back against a narrow head and an ugly stump of a tail.

Justin took no notice of him.

" Come on," he said, " let's go."

If there was any question of a debt, he thought, which there was not, nor ever had been, but still, if there was one, he was about to discharge it in full.

Grace, still in the car, looked up at him.

" You aren't going to repeat those things I said, are you ? "

" No," he said.

" You know I'm grateful, don't you ? There's something so reassuring about your being here that I'm almost surprised. This having known each other for such years, it seems to mean something." It sounded as if she were trying more, but could not.

He was as unable to respond directly.

" This dog's an ugly beast," he said. " For some reason, I seem to think I've seen him somewhere."

" It's Brillhart's." Grace got out of the car. " And it probably means Brillhart's around. The dog's always with him."

" Who's Brillhart ? "

" A man who works for Arnold. Hester must have telephoned him too. I should have expected that."

They walked towards the house.

At the first few steps they took, the dog barked angrily, then, as they continued, retreated slowly backwards, snarling.

" If a dog's savage, it's its owner's fault," Grace said. " It's just like Brillhart to have a savage dog."

" Brillhart's someone you don't like ? "

" No."

" Why not ? "

" He's a liar."

" Aren't we all ? "

They had reached the circular porch that jutted out from the front of the house. Mounting the few steps to it, they found themselves again sheltered from the rain.

Grace tossed her dark hair back from her face and rubbed the back of her hand across her damp forehead.

" I used to like him," she said. " I used to believe the things he told me. That's why I dislike him now as much as I do. I wish he weren't here, but I ought to have known that Hester would send for him at once. I ought to have realised she'd have done that before she telephoned me. Possibly if I'd thought of that sooner . . ."

" Wouldn't you have come ? "

" Oh, I'd have come. I had to come."

" Well, then ? "

" I'd have got here quicker," she muttered hurriedly, as steps approached them from the other side of the door.

It was opened by a constable, a tall elderly man who recognised Grace.

" Evening, Mrs. DeLong," he said. " Mrs. Thaine's expecting you."

But instead of letting them in, he looked questioningly at Justin.

" This is Mr. Emery," Grace said. " An old friend of mine, who's visiting me."

The constable let them come in then.

" That dog," he said, as he closed the door quickly after them so that the dog was shut out, " he's been making a nuisance of himself all the evening. Snarls at everyone, but won't go home. If he was mine, I'd soon teach him to mind his own business."

" Why don't you get Mr. Brillhart to do something about him ? " Grace asked. "That barking will get on our nerves."

" He isn't here," the constable said.

" Where is he, then ? Why's the dog here ? "

" I couldn't say, ma'am."

" Where's Mrs. Thaine ? "

" I'm here," a woman's voice answered from a doorway.

Justin turned his head sharply, for he had heard no footsteps.

Hester Thaine was standing there, her arms spread out across the doorway, her hands gripping the sides of it, as if she needed that support to keep her upright.

Justin's first impression of her was that she was tall, but this was mostly because the doorways in the old house were so low that her head was not many inches away from the lintel, and also because of her extreme slenderness. She was far too slender, a wraith of a woman, with the look of there being scarcely room inside her for all the usual bones and organs. Her pallor and her soft, fair hair, looped loosely back from her face and worn in a knot on her neck, and a dress of an indeterminate grey-green colour, of some flimsy material, which here and there let through the glow of the firelight from the room behind her, helped to make her seem insubstantial and almost ghost-like. But her eyes were brilliant and alive. There were no signs that she had been crying, but in her drawn, pale face they shone with a feverish brightness.

Grace went to her quickly, lifting her arms towards her as if she were about to embrace her. But as Hester Thaine made no movement, staying in the doorway, gripping both doorposts, Grace stood still before her, looking rather helpless and quite uncertain what to say or do next. Then she remembered Justin and beckoned him forward.

" This is Justin Emery," she said. " I know I've told you about him. He happened to be visiting me, so I brought him over. I thought—I thought he might be able to help."

It was the second time that Grace had deliberately given the impression that Justin was staying at her house. The first time he had scarcely noted it, but with the repetition, he began to wonder what her motive was.

Hester turned her burning eyes on Justin. The look in them hurt him. There was such an intensity of pain in them that it seemed to overflow into him.

" Thank you, Mr. Emery, it was kind of you to come," she said in a light, formal, unnatural voice.

He answered quickly, " I was afraid of only being in the

way. You can't really want a stranger here at the moment."

" The house is full of strangers."

Turning, she went back into the drawing-room.

Grace and Justin followed her in. A big fire was blazing
on the hearth and nearly all the light in the room came from
the flames, for the only lamp that had been lit was one on a
desk in a corner.

Some papers were spread out in the pool of light on the
desk, which was of cherry-wood and probably early-Victorian,
like the rest of the furniture in the room. Though Justin
was not in a mood to notice details, it struck him as strange,
even then, as he went towards the fire, that the Thaines'
drawing-room should so obviously contain not one piece of
furniture designed by Arnold Thaine.

" By strangers, I suppose you mean the police," Grace
said.

She did not sit down when Hester dropped exhaustedly
into a deep, velvet-covered chair, but remained standing in
the middle of the room, looking as if there were something
somewhere else to which she must attend in a moment.

" Yes, the police," Hester said. " And the doctor. They're
all—out there." She made a slight motion with her head
towards the window.

" In the studio ? "

" Yes."

" That's where it happened ? "

" Yes."

Justin, bemused and uncomfortable, watched the two
women, rather wishing that some policeman would come
into the room, to bring an official and impersonal element
into it.

He guessed that Hester Thaine was in a state of extreme
shock. He guessed also that she was hardly aware of his
presence or Grace's, and that if Grace were to proceed with
the questions that were bursting from her, she would very
likely receive answers so automatic that Hester afterwards
might not even remember having given them. Alternatively,
Grace might be met by a stupefied silence, or provoke a
collapse.

Hoping intensely that she would not risk this, Justin felt for his cigarettes in his pocket, then withdrew his hand, remembering that he had not been invited to smoke. As he did so, he found Hester Thaine's eyes upon him. Though they shone so feverishly, they were not unaware of him. They were taking him in with a rather puzzled but eager interest, as if he were in some way of great importance in the situation.

"Please smoke, Mr. Emery," she said in her formal, quiet voice. She turned to Grace. "I know you want to know it all and I'll tell you what I can."

"Don't talk if you don't want to," Grace said. She sat down abruptly on the arm of a chair, but still kept the air of being ready to hurry from the room.

"I do want to," Hester answered. "I want to tell it all to you, then—then, if you don't mind, you can tell it to the others."

"Brillhart?"

"Yes, and Ben. And anyone else."

"Hasn't Brillhart been here?"

"I don't know where he is," Hester said. "I telephoned, but no one answered."

"But the dog . . ."

"I know, it's queer. He was shut up in the house when I got here."

"Then Brillhart must have been here."

"Perhaps. I don't know. The dog was shut up in the kitchen, howling. It was horrible. I've never liked that dog."

"No one does except Brillhart. And that's his fault, or rather, his intention."

Hester gave Grace a quick look, then looked at Justin, then dropped her eyes.

"It was around nine o'clock when I got in," she said. "I'd been in Wallport as usual, shopping, but I got back rather later than I usually do, because I went to a film. The house was all dark and the dog was howling. But the lights were on in the studio, so I didn't really think of anything being wrong. I turned the dog out and I tried to telephone

Brillhart about him. But there wasn't any answer. So then I changed my dress and started getting supper. When it was ready, I gave Arnold a ring in the studio and there wasn't any answer from him either. That was when I began to worry, though I didn't think—I didn't guess——" Her voice dried up harshly in her throat.

" Of course you didn't," Grace said. " You just thought perhaps he'd gone out or something."

Hester hesitated, then nodded. Justin did not think that that was what she had thought at all.

She cleared her throat and went on, " I went to the studio then and I found him. He was on the floor. He was dead and quite cold. He must have been lying there for hours. All the time I was in the cinema. Hours."

" What did you do ? " Grace asked.

" I'm not sure," Hester said. " Really, I'm not sure. I didn't understand how he could be dead. I didn't even understand just then that he'd been shot. But the police say I told them on the telephone that he'd been shot. Perhaps I did."

" There wasn't any gun in the room ? "

" I don't think so."

" You didn't look ? "

" No, I don't think I stayed in the room more than a minute or two. I always hated it."

" I know," Grace said, with an emphasis that caught Justin's attention.

" The first thing I remember properly is talking to the police on the telephone," Hester said. " Then I came in here and waited. That dog went on howling outside and I couldn't bear it, so then I telephoned you."

" And Brillhart."

" Yes. I tried again but he still wasn't there."

" What about Ben ? Does he know ? "

" No."

All at once, Grace looked angry. " Why haven't you told him ? "

" How could he help ? "

" But he ought to know. He'd want to know."

" Then you tell him."

The two women exchanged a long, intent look.

Grace turned her head to look at the telephone. It was on the cherry-wood desk, in the circle of light cast by the reading-lamp.

She seemed about to do what Hester had suggested, but as if the sight of the telephone itself had some effect upon her, an undecided look appeared on her face.

" Shall I try ringing Brillhart again, to tell him to come and take his dog away ? " she suggested.

Hester said nothing.

Grace stood up and perfunctorily, as a person will who is not really expecting an answer, dialled a number.

Justin heard a buzz, then immediately the muttering sound of a voice replying to the ring.

" Lewis ? " Grace said. " This is Grace. I'm at the Thaines'. Your dog's here."

An excited voice poured a torrent of words into her ear.

" All right," she interrupted. " He's here, he's quite safe, so suppose you come and get him."

There was more excitable speech from the other end of the line.

" Yes, now, of course," Grace replied impatiently and put the telephone down. She turned to Hester again. " He said he thought the dog was lost. He's in a ridiculous state about it. As if that brute couldn't take care of itself. Now I think I'll go and talk to the police. I want to tell them . . . I want to ask them . . ." Instead of finishing, she went quickly out of the room.

Hester, looking after her but still saying nothing, had a startled gleam in her eyes. Something had just happened that had taken her quite by surprise. Then suddenly she bent her head and covered her face with her thin, long-fingered hands.

Justin did not think that she was crying. She sat too still for that.

While they stayed there, opposite to one another, in silence, he noticed how the firelight glinted on her soft, fine-textured hair and the transparent folds of her dress.

Under the silk there was some heavy lace of the same colour as the silk and shot with a metallic thread. The dress was a beautiful one, but strangely sumptuous for a woman who, according to her own story, had come in from marketing to cook the supper for herself and her husband.

Presently Hester raised her head and looked at him thoughtfully.

" She didn't tell him about Arnold," she said.

" No," he agreed.

" It was like setting a trap ? "

" It was, rather."

" I didn't like that."

" I could see you didn't."

" Do you know Lewis Brillhart ? "

" No."

She gave a sigh. " I'm very fond of him. And so was Arnold. But you'd think Grace hated him, wouldn't you, from the way she spoke of him ? "

" She's very upset," Justin said.

" Of course. But she could have told him. . . . You've known Grace a long time, haven't you, Mr. Emery ? "

" Most of my life."

" What's she really like, then ? Does she change her mind very suddenly about people ? Are they her dearest friends one day and her enemies the next ? Is she one of those people ? "

" I don't think so," he said. " No. I think she's rather more loyal than most people, in her way."

" I think she used to like me," Hester went on, " but now I often have the feeling that she can't bear me, and I don't know why, because I'm sure I haven't changed. And I know she used to like Lewis. You know, it was she who introduced him to us a couple of years ago. And she'd never have praised him as she did if she hadn't meant it. She's very honest. But now—now she thinks he murdered Arnold."

" And you ? " Justin said. " What do you think ? "

" Oh, it must have been a tramp, a burglar."

" I suppose so."

"You see, though I wouldn't say he had no enemies, the sort of enemies a man like Arnold has aren't the sort of people who do murder."

Justin nodded, because it seemed impossible at such a time to do anything but agree with everything she said, but his forehead creased in an unconscious frown and she saw it.

"Then you don't think so," she said. "But why? What has Grace been saying?"

"Nothing much. She was too shocked to say much."

"Yes, of course. Though sometimes that's just when one says most. Didn't she say . . . ?" She stopped. Her eyes, as she gazed at him, widened in a look of deepening terror. In a low, surprised tone, she added, "It would be very easy to say too much to you. Do you know that about yourself?"

He answered uneasily, "There's no need for you to worry about anything you've said."

"No, but all the same. . . . I was going to tell you something about Ben Eagan. Nothing that matters, yet not knowing him, you might have thought . . . It isn't important, anyway."

Again she bent her head and covered her face in her hands.

IV

SOON AFTERWARDS Justin saw the room full of clocks.

This was at his own request. But it was a request no sooner made than he regretted it. Driven to it less by curiosity than by some anxiety for which he could not wholly account, though he knew that it concerned Grace and that it made him feel that it was imperative for him to learn all that he could of the crime, he found, as soon as he was taken into Arnold Thaine's studio, that he had only one desire, which was to get out of it again as quickly as possible.

This was not because the body of Arnold Thaine still lay where the murderer had left it. Justin had seen death many times and in itself it moved him less than, privately, he thought it ought. He was able to look at the big, sprawled body on the floor of the studio and meet the glare of the blue eyes in the white, agonised, handsome face with very little revulsion and with what was more like a disturbed sense of apology than pity.

Death, Detective-Inspector Turkis told him, had been instantaneous. But there were three bullets in the body and a fourth, that had gone wide of its target, had embedded itself in a clock that hung on the wall above the fireplace.

This clock was the only one in the room that was not going. Its heavy pendulum hung still. The time at which its ornately moulded hands pointed was five minutes past one.

" Just look at that, will you ! " Turkis muttered. He was a big, burly man with a square-jawed, stubborn face and reflective eyes. " That clock could have told us the exact minute when the crime was committed if only Thaine had ever bothered to set his clocks. But it seems that didn't interest him. There isn't one in the room that's even nearly correct."

" What about his own watch ? " Justin asked.

" He didn't wear one."

"That wrist-watch on the table with the broken strap . . . ?"

" It isn't his. And it's stopped too—at ten-twenty-nine."

Justin looked up once more at the clock that had stopped. It was a very old clock, or a good imitation of an old one, of the type that he thought of vaguely as being called a lantern-clock. If it was genuine, he supposed, it was valuable.

" About what time was the crime committed ? " he asked.

" The doctor says roughly between three and five-thirty," Turkis answered.

Justin glanced round at the rest of the clocks. There were two tall grandfathers, each in a corner of the room. There was a frivolous arrangement of cupids under a glass bell. There was a curious clock with only one hand that seemed to require a trickle of water to keep it going. There were all kinds of other clocks, including a brisk little modern clock on the table at which Arnold Thaine had apparently been working when his murderer came into the room. Looking at this clock, Justin felt a sudden and overpowering aversion to the whole place.

It was the sort of feeling that can be roused, in inexplicable violence, by contact with perversion. If only that one clock, that little modern clock, that must have faced Thaine as he stooped over the drawings spread out on the table, had told the time correctly, the meaning of the whole room would somehow have been changed. But even that clock, its ticking merging with that of all the others in a chattering sound, not unlike voices at a party, heard at a little distance, announced the time at that moment to be three-nineteen.

" Liars," Justin muttered explosively. " Liars, every one of them."

" I beg your pardon," Turkis said.

Justin did not repeat it.

" This room would drive me mad if I had to stay in it," he said

" Me too."

" I wonder if conceivably the shot in that clock could have been sheer mockery."

" That's putting in words something I've had in my mind," Turkis said, " but I'd sooner think it was just the shot that missed. Seen all you want to now ? "

" More than I want to, thanks." Justin turned towards the door. " Now I've got the feeling I'm really mixed up in the damn' business. Before, I was only a visitor."

" You were mixed up in it before, like it or not," Turkis said. " No one pays visits on murder for politeness' sake."

They left the studio together.

The rain had stopped by now. There was a dripping from the low eaves of the studio into the sodden grass of the lawn, but the night, though it was as dark as ever, had grown quiet.

" You're quite right, of course," Justin said, rather bitterly, thinking how easily, that morning, he might have decided against coming to Archersfield at all.

" Naturally, I know why you came," Turkis said. " But you'll find it doesn't end there."

Abruptly he walked off, going towards a corner of the

house, round which a group of men, dark, uniformed figures with bull's-eye lamps, had just appeared.

Justin stood still for a moment, frowning as he thought over what Turkis had said. Then he returned to the house. He went back to the drawing-room, where he found Grace and Hester talking together in low voices, which ceased as he came in. Both looked up with questions in their eyes.

" You were a long time," Grace said. " What had they to ask you ? "

" Just my name and address and so on," Justin said.

" You were a long time," Grace repeated.

" And they took you out there," Hester said, with a movement of her head in the direction of the studio. " Why did they do that ? "

" I asked them to," he said.

Grace asked sharply, " Why ? "

Instead of answering, he looked uncertainly at Hester.

" I hope you don't mind, Mrs. Thaine," he said. " I know I'd no business there."

She shook her head, but there was a perplexed frown between her eyes.

Grace asked her question again, " Why, Justin ? "

" Perhaps just curiosity," he said, " or an idea that it might come in useful."

She gave him a hard stare, full of dissatisfaction.

" I told them about coming here this morning and finding no one in," she said. " Hester, of course, was in Wallport. She doesn't know why Arnold was out then."

" This morning ? " Justin said. " I thought you said——"

" Yes, don't you remember ? Before you arrived. Don't you remember, when you got off the bus, I wasn't there ? I told you it was because I'd been to the Thaines."

" Oh, yes."

He saw that she had deliberately dragged in the subject of her earlier visit as a way of informing him that she had told the police nothing of the later one, and also as a way of warning him not to mention that second visit in front of Hester.

The folly of it disturbed him so much that he grew angry and turned away, scowling, to the fire. But he could still feel Grace watching him.

"No, I don't know where Arnold can have been this morning," Hester said. ' I didn't know he meant to go out. He doesn't—he didn't—usually. He nearly always spent the whole morning working here, then went to the workshop in the afternoon. But it can't be important, anyway. I know he was home by lunch-time, because he ate the lunch I left for him and made himself some coffee. . . ." She stopped as a louder barking and yelping broke out in the garden. "That's Brillhart," she said.

Grace stood up abruptly. Hester rose too. Justin realised that her thin figure, beside Grace's stocky one, was tense with some fear or expectancy. Grace gave her a sidelong look, then drew away from her. A moment later the door opened and a man came in.

He came in in a rush and taking absolutely no notice of the presence of Grace or Justin in the room, strode straight to Hester, holding out both his hands and clasping hers.

"What is it, Hester? All these police! In God's name, what's happened?"

He was a man of about fifty, rather below the average in height, but heavily built. He had a large, square head, covered in thick, crisply curling grey hair and set on a thick neck between wide, muscular shoulders. His eyes were blue and slightly prominent and his features were heavy, but with an unusual mobility and expressiveness. What they expressed just then, apart from an intense anxiety, as his eyes gazed into Hester Thaine's, was so blatant that Justin was momentarily taken aback. Nothing that either of the women had said had led him to expect that this man whom they had been discussing would turn out to be so passionately and openly in love with Hester.

Hester withdrew her hands from Brillhart's and clasped them behind her.

"It's Arnold," she said. Her colour had risen slightly. "He's——"

"He's been murdered," Grace said loudly.

Lewis Brillhart did not even seem to hear her.

" Hester, tell me ! "

" Yes, it's true," Hester said, almost inaudibly. " Arnold's dead. Someone got into the studio when he was there alone and shot him. It's true, it's murder."

" Oh God, oh God ! " Brillhart cried on a rising note of feverish excitement. " Not Arnold—I can't believe it ! It can't be true ! Oh God, how could such a thing happen ? " His face had flushed a deep red and he had started to tremble.

" Yes, Lewis," Hester said.

Brillhart swung round on Grace.

" And you—you telephoned. You telephoned, but you said nothing of this ! "

Grace replied with cold composure, " I telephoned to ask you to come and remove your dog, because the noise he makes has been getting badly on our nerves. And if you would now remove him as quickly as possible, I think we should all be grateful."

Outside the dog howled again. Hester shuddered and edged nearer to the fire, farther away from Brillhart.

As he glanced round at her, his face showed everything he felt so nakedly that to Justin it was embarrassing to see it. There was a kind of childishness in Brillhart's expression, an innocence and an exaggeration of both love and anger, that to one of Justin's temperament made the man seem exceedingly strange.

" I wonder if you know what it's like to be hated as you seem to hate me," Brillhart said in a choking voice to Grace. " I wonder what I've done. And I wonder if perhaps you don't suffer from it at least as much as I do."

Grace's tone remained cold and level. " D'you know that Hester found your dog shut up in the house here when she got back from Wallport—and found Arnold dead ? How do you explain that ? "

" Grace—please ! " Hester said. " Lewis, I haven't yet introduced Mr. Emery, a friend of Grace's."

For the first time Brillhart looked at Justin.

" Forgive me," he said. " Of course I saw you, but my

mind's all confused. I can't think, I can't believe . . ." He gave up the effort to talk to the stranger and turned back to Hester. " Can you tell me what's happening ? Please try to, if you're able, before Grace actually accuses me of committing a murder that I still know nothing about."

Justin found Hester's eyes lifted imploringly to him. In a few sentences, he told Brillhart the story that Hester had told of her return from Wallport and her finding the dead body of her husband.

Before he had quite finished, Grace interrupted, " Well, Lewis, how did the dog get in here ? "

" The dog, the dog ! " Brillhart exploded. " The dog was lost. I told you that on the telephone. I left him shut up in the yard when I went out this morning. Someone must have come in and let him out."

" Why did you leave him shut up in the yard ? " Grace asked. " I thought you always took him to the workshop with you."

" I didn't go to the workshop to-day. I went to London. I went up by the six-twenty this morning and I got back only a few minutes before you telephoned. I found the yard door was wide open and the dog gone. Well, Grace, go on, won't you ? Go on and ask me as many more impertinent questions as you want to."

She gave a heavy sigh. " I don't mean to be impertinent, Lewis."

There was a faint note of conciliation in it. Immediately the look on Brillhart's heavy, expressive features changed. The anger and defiance were replaced by an eager, emotional friendliness.

" No, of course not—no, I shouldn't have said impertinent. And you and I shouldn't quarrel, Grace—not you and I. I know you only want to know the truth. And I should like to know that too. I'd like to know who let my dog out and who brought him here. He doesn't follow strangers."

" I expect it was an accident," Hester said, " and nothing at all to do with Arnold's death. For all we know, Arnold brought him here himself."

" Did Arnold go to my house, then ? " Brillhart asked.
" Why should he have done that ? "

" I was only guessing," Hester said and sank down again
into the chair by the fire, doing it so suddenly that it looked
almost as if her legs had given way beneath her.

Twisting sideways in the chair, she leant one cheek
against the velvet and closed her eyes. There was a kind
of protest in the attitude, a demand on them all to be quiet,
to ask no more questions, to save their doubts and suspicions
for later.

It brought a silence upon them.

After a moment, however, Grace said uncertainly,
" Hester, what are you going to do about to-night ? Would
you like to come home with me ? "

" That's very kind of you," Hester said without opening
her eyes. " But I think, no, I'll stay here."

" I'd be glad to have you."

" I know. Thank you. But you understand, don't you ? "

A look appeared on Grace's face that Justin did not much
care for. It was as if she thought she understood too well.

" Well then," she said, " since Lewis is here to look after
you now, I think Justin and I might perhaps be going—
unless we can still help in any way."

Hester again murmured thanks, but made no effort to
persuade her to stay.

Grace looked at Justin. " I suppose we have to ask the
police if we may leave."

" The police ! " Brillhart cried and slapped his palm
against his forehead. " They're going to insist in inter-
viewing me, aren't they ? "

" They are," Grace said as she went to the door. " I hope
you can prove to them that you were really in London."

Outside the house, in the darkness, Brillhart's dog leapt
at Justin, barking and growling. Justin raised a threatening
arm and the dog stood still.

The night was pitch dark, smelling of wet earth and rotted
leaves.

Grace shivered.

" Will you come home with me and have a drink, or d'you

want me to drive you straight back to your hotel ? " she
asked.

" D'you want me to go home with you ? "

" Yes."

" All right, then."

" But there's something I want to do first," she said, as
they went to the car, the dog following them suspiciously at
a slight distance, " I want to see Ben Eagan."

V

BEN EAGAN lived in a cottage on a lonely stretch of road
about a quarter of a mile from Fallow Corner. When Grace
and Justin drove up to the cottage, all the windows were
dark except one, in which a light shone behind dark red
curtains.

When Grace knocked, a young man in pyjamas and an old
dressing-gown came to the door, looked at them in a puzzled
way and said vaguely, " Oh, hallo, Grace."

" Did we wake you up ? " she asked.

" No," he said, " I was reading. What time is it ? "

" D'you still not know ? "

This struck Justin, when he thought it over, as a curious
question.

" No," Ben Eagan replied to it, " I meant to set the kitchen
clock going this morning when I got back, but I forgot. Is
it very late ? "

" It's ten past one," Grace said. " Late for a visit. But
aren't you going to ask us in all the same ? This is Justin
Emery, an old friend of mine. We've got to talk to you."

Eagan showed no surprise at the lateness of the hour.
Saying, " Oh, sorry," he stood aside to let them in.

He took them into a small bed-sitting-room, which besides
being supremely untidy, was unswept and undusted. The
appearance of the bed showed that it had been made by
pulling the blankets up roughly over the tumbled pillows

then throwing a crumpled cotton counterpane crookedly over them. Unwashed tea-cups and glasses were stacked on a small table.

As if he considered that Grace understood the situation, but that a stranger required to have it explained to him, Eagan turned to Justin, saying with a slightly embarrassed smile, " I'm afraid it's an awful mess. My landlady's in hospital."

" I told you you'd never manage by yourself," Grace said. " You're no Brillhart. You ought to have come to stay with me, as I suggested."

Eagan gave another embarrassed smile. He was about thirty, a tall, slender young man with a slight stoop and a certain tentativeness and slowness in his movements. His hair and his eyes were dark, but his skin was fair, with very little colour. In a nervous, absent way, he looked intelligent and though his features were a little too fine-drawn, with marks of an over-sensitiveness of temperament, his hesitant smile had great charm.

" I've got some beer," he said. " Would you like some ? Or shall I make some tea ? " As he spoke, he looked dubiously at the unwashed cups and glasses.

" Don't bother," Grace said. " We aren't staying." She was standing with her back to the fire, having shaken her head briefly at the chair that Eagan had started to clear of books and papers. " Ben, have you heard about Arnold ? "

" Heard what ? " he asked as vaguely as before.

" You haven't heard that—that he's dead—that he's been murdered ? "

He stared at her uncomprehendingly.

In short, dry sentences, she told him of the events of that night.

Eagan stood quite still while she spoke, except that his fingers started to pluck at the cord of his dressing-gown. There was very little expression on his face, though the pale skin seemed to tighten over the bones behind it. Justin thought that he knew what type of man Eagan was. They looked so nervous and unstable, that type, yet in a crisis they were steady as rocks, showing practically no emotion at all. But presently Eagan would go suddenly from the room and be sick.

When Grace had stopped speaking, Eagan said in a low, hurried voice, " I'd better go there at once. I'd better go to Hester."

" I shouldn't," Grace said.

" Yes," he said, " I'll go. She ought to have someone with her."

" She's got Brillhart." This was said with an added intentness in the gaze that Grace kept on the young man's face.

He only muttered, " He's no use."

" All the same, she telephoned to him and not to you," Grace said.

Eagan seemed not to notice the sudden brutality in her tone.

" But he always loses his head at the first chance," he said.

" Oh no, not Brillhart."

" Yes, he can never think straight about anything. I'd better go. If you don't mind . . ." His hands went to the cord of his dressing-gown again, showing that he was in haste for them to leave so that he could dress.

Grace gave a determined shake of her head. " Wait till the morning," she said. " Wait till she sends for you herself."

Justin was puzzled. He felt that there was more in Grace's determination that Eagan should not go to Hester Thaine than simple concern for Hester's feelings. Her determination came, he felt, out of something that was between herself and Eagan. It made Justin wish that she would let the young man make up his own mind.

She went on, " She will send for you, of course. But she doesn't want you there now. I know."

Eagan frowned uncertainly.

" If you go there now," she said, " the police are going to start questioning you."

" What about ? " he asked.

" About whether or not you saw Arnold to-day ? "

" Oh yes. Well, I don't mind telling them about that."

" Did you see him ? You told me you didn't."

" That was this morning. I saw him in the afternoon."

Her eyes widened. The words, which Eagan had spoken quite casually, seemed to have given her an intense shock. " When ? " she asked, suddenly hoarse.

Eagan began to look annoyed.

" I haven't any idea. I told you this morning, I bust my watch. The strap broke and it fell on the floor and stopped. And I'd let the kitchen clock here run down after Mrs. Bell was taken to hospital. So it could have been any time."

" Not quite any time. You must have known roughly. You must have known if it was getting dark already, or if it got dark fairly soon after you got home. You must be able to make a guess."

" What's the use of a guess ? " He was looking resentful.

" Well, was it getting dark ? "

" No, it wasn't. It didn't get dark for quite a time after I got back."

" So it must have been quite early in the afternoon when you saw Arnold."

" I suppose so, yes."

" You know your watch is there on the table in the studio ? "

" I'd imagine it would be. I put it there."

" I haven't told the police it was yours. I imagine Hester hasn't either."

A sharp exclamation broke from Eagan. Then he threw himself down in a chair.

Justin, embarrassed at Grace's attitude and uncomfortable at the rising anger in Eagan, turned away from them and as he did so, his gaze chanced to slide across a sheet of paper that lay, with an uncapped fountain-pen, on a table. A few words, written in a clear and unusually fine handwriting, leapt up at him from the paper.

" Dear Arnold, after our conversation, I think the only thing for me to do is to resign . . ."

There was more of it, but by the time Justin had taken in so much, he had obeyed the tabu that had been instilled in him since he had first learnt to read and had averted his eyes.

Eagan was saying, " I can't imagine why you didn't tell the police the watch was mine, if they wanted to know."

" They didn't ask me directly," Grace said.

That letter, Justin thought, might be something important. He ought to have read the rest of it while he had the chance. But to do it now deliberately, without being observed by Eagan, felt impossible.

" And I didn't want to add any complications to the situation," Grace added. " Was Arnold going to mend your watch for you ? "

" Yes," Eagan said. " What d'you mean by complications ? "

" Oh, it was just in case—in case——" She stumbled and her tired face flushed a little. " What did you and Arnold talk about this afternoon ? "

Eagan did not answer, but his eyes told her that what he and Thaine had discussed that afternoon was not her business.

After a pause, he said, " I don't understand you. D'you think I've some connection with this murder ? " His voice was hard and dry and inexpressive.

Grace frowned as if she found him stupid. " No, but I thought I'd just warn you . . ."

" I don't need any warning."

" And I wanted to ask you," she went on hurriedly, as if she were trying to cover up a mistake, " did Arnold say anything to you about expecting anyone else to come and see him ? Because, you see, you may have been the last person before the murderer to see Arnold alive."

" I don't think he said anything like that," Eagan said. " I don't remember it, if he did. We talked about other things."

" And he said he'd mend your watch for you ? "

" Yes."

She gave a deep sigh and turned towards the door.

It made Eagan speak quickly. " Grace—you've got some idea about all this, haven't you ? "

She shook her head with intense weariness.

"Yes," he said, "you've been asking me all these questions for a reason."

"I haven't, Ben," she said. "It was only to see if you could give me an idea. Coming, Justin?"

Justin was glad to go.

She spoke again over her shoulder to Eagan, "You aren't going round there now, are you?"

"No," he said, "but I'll go first thing in the morning, whether Hester sends for me or not. I think she will send for me."

"While Brillhart's there?"

She went out.

As Justin followed her, he saw Eagan's face suddenly redden in anger and his eyes grow furious.

Grace drove the short distance to her house in silence. When they reached it, she took Justin into the cold kitchen and set about making tea. Her face, all the while, was bleak and abstracted.

In the quiet house, the ticking of a clock on the kitchen wall sounded noisy and assertive. Sitting down, leaning his elbows on the scrubbed top of the table, Justin compared the clock with his own watch and saw with relief that they both showed the same time to the minute. Here, at least, was a clock that was doing what a clock should do.

"Your hotel will be all locked up," Grace said presently. "You'd better stay on here. Or d'you worry about the proprieties, like Ben? I was quite ready to look after him when his landlady went to hospital, but he wouldn't hear of it."

"Could be that wasn't because of the proprieties."

"What was it, then?"

Justin struggled with a yawn. He had suddenly become unbearably tired.

"Some people just like being independent," he said.

"Not Ben. Look at the mess he's got into."

"He may not mind a mess."

She shook her head impatiently. "Brillhart, now. He lives alone all the time, but then he can cook and sew and he keeps his house much better than I do. But Ben was just afraid." She turned away, making a clumsy gesture with one hand as she did so, which knocked the lid off the boiling kettle. " He thinks—oh, stupid things."

Justin looked at her curiously. " True things ? " he asked.

Patches of red appeared on the back of her neck, but when she turned towards him, her face was pale and frowning.

" Just stupid. He's very young and ignorant, although he's so brilliant at his work."

" Why were you asking him all those questions ? To find out if he could know that you'd been to the Thaines' house in the afternoon yourself ? "

She took a long time to answer, then said almost absently, " I wonder, after all, if I like you as much as I used to. I thought, as soon as we met, that you'd changed. One used to be able to trust you to have a certain sort of insight."

He stuck to his own line of thought. " You didn't tell the police about that afternoon visit of yours, did you ? "

" No."

" Then you must be very anxious to make sure that nobody saw you."

" Nobody did see me."

" You can't ever be sure. I wish you'd told the police the facts straight away. You'll have to, sometime."

" Why ? My visit had nothing to do with all this."

" Then why make a secret of it ? "

" Because—because——" She turned back to the stove, pouring the boiling water into the teapot.

" Why did you go there, Grace ? " Justin asked.

She did not answer.

He tried again. " And where do you come into it all ? "

" I don't," she said. Putting the teapot on the table, she sat down opposite him. A profound dejection took all sound of evasiveness out of her words. " I don't come in anywhere. Couldn't you see that ? "

" But you must," he said. " You have to belong in it somewhere. Brillhart, Eagan, Thaine, Hester Thaine— and you."

" No," she said, " I don't come in at all."

He went on reflectively, " Thaine's murdered. And Brillhart's in love with Thaine's wife. It sounds simple. And you suspect Brillhart of the murder. But then you find out that Brillhart spent the day in London. So you think of Eagan. But you seem to like Eagan. All the same, you go out of your way to make him believe that Brillhart's going to spend the night with Mrs. Thaine, the night right after her husband's been murdered——"

" No," she broke in, " you've got it all wrong. For one thing, Brillhart isn't in love with Hester."

" Good God, but the way he looked at her ! "

" He looks at every woman like that."

" Not just like that, Grace."

" Yes, really—particularly if he depends on her to some extent for his bread and butter."

" That's a hard thing to say."

" All right, it's hard."

" And Hester ? What does she feel about him."

" I don't know. That's something I can't make out. I wish I could, because it was I who thrust Brillhart on the Thaines, so now I feel responsible."

He sipped some tea. " Tell me, does she dress like that every evening ? "

Grace looked surprised and then amused by the question.

" That's Arnold," she explained. " He thought it a very important part of a woman's life to be beautiful all the time and poor Hester really worked at it. It would have driven me mad. There were a lot of things about Arnold that would have driven me mad if I'd had to live with them. Yet I did like him. He was so talented and so honest. An awful bully, I suppose, but with nothing cheap or squalid about him. Really a rather great man, and they aren't common."

" And what did Hester think about it all ? "

" You keep on asking me questions about Hester. I told you, I don't understand her. I think she was in love with him. I know she always tried very hard to please him. Per-

haps too hard for it to be quite real, I don't know. I know
I'd never try so hard with anyone I really loved. But Hester
and I aren't in the least alike, not in any way."

He let it go at that, making no further effort to resist his
tiredness. The hot tea was good. He let his thoughts dwell
on the image of Hester Thaine, sitting in the firelight wearing
the soft, shimmering dress that she had put on to please her
demanding husband.

Presently Justin realised that Grace had just addressed a
question to him. He had to ask her to repeat it.

"Marion," she said, "Marion Garston—why don't you
go to see her?"

"Oh no," he said.

"Why not?"

"Why should I? If I don't mean anything to her."

"I think you do."

"Then I don't want to."

"Why not?"

"Oh, it's so long ago."

"It's just as long ago that you last saw me, yet you come
here."

"That's a different thing."

Her face contracted slightly, almost as if it were in some
way painful that it should be so different. But she said,
"I'm glad you came. Only, as it's turned out, it isn't
going to be any fun for you, poor Justin."

"No," he agreed, "murder isn't any fun."

"Of course," she went on, looking at him abstractedly,
"Brillhart did it. The only question is, how."

"How he shot a man who was ninety miles away?"

'That's it."

"I think," Justin said, "there must be one or two other
questions besides that."

VI

NEXT MORNING two detectives called at Fallow Corner.

Justin, who had had difficulty in getting to sleep and then had slept late, heard their voices downstairs while he still lay in bed.

A few minutes afterwards, he heard a peremptory knock on his door.

"That man Turkis is here," Grace said softly outside it. "Come down as quickly as you can."

Something in her voice told Justin that she had just had a shock of some kind and that her demand was urgent. Getting up and dressing rapidly, he went downstairs and found Grace with Turkis and another detective in the sitting-room. In Grace's face, as she stood by the newly kindled fire, which as yet had scarcely started to warm the room, Justin saw what he had heard upstairs in her voice. She was frightened. Yet there was nothing menacing in Turkis's expression, but only a troubled and tired-eyed look of inquiry.

"Will you tell Mr. Emery what you've just told me," Grace said to him, trying hard to look and sound normal. The effort increased the slight harshness and arrogance that there usually was in her voice.

Turkis turned to Justin. "I came to tell Mrs. DeLong about some information we've picked up," he said, "because I wondered if perhaps she mightn't be able to add something to it. I thought she might have some ideas about it that could help us."

"But I haven't," Grace said. "I've told the inspector I haven't any idea who the two women could be."

With a sinking of his heart, Justin realised that she was warning him, just as she had the evening before when Hester Thaine had been there, not to say any more in answer to any questions that he might be asked than she had chosen to say.

48

The stupidity, the sheer wrongness of it, made Justin for the moment so angry with her that his expression, as he met Turkis's look, appeared to be one of extreme irritation with the inspector himself.

" If Mrs. DeLong can't help you," he said, " I don't suppose I can. But I'd like to hear what your information is."

" It's like this," Turkis said. " There's a cottage near to the Thaines' house where a couple live who've got their old grandfather living with them. Both the young people are out all day at work. He's a gardener and she's cook at the Crown Hotel in Archersfield. The old grandfather's mostly bedridden. When the young folk go out in the morning, they fix him up in a chair by the kitchen window, so that he can amuse himself, watching anyone who goes by, and they put the wireless near him and his dinner where he's only got to reach out and take it. Well, yesterday, because of the rain, the old man decided not to sit by the window. He decided he'd stay in bed. And it just so happens that his bedroom window faces straight across a small meadow to the Thaines' house."

" And he saw several people go in and out during the afternoon," Grace broke in. " A man and two women. And he knows at just what time each of them did it, because he'd got his wireless on all the time and he remembers, or thinks he does, about when, in each programme, each person went in and out."

" So you've at last found someone hereabouts who's interested in time," Justin said.

Turkis smiled briefly.

" It doesn't help much," he said. " It isn't the times I'm interested in at the moment, but simply who those people were. The first one, the man, at around three-thirty, was Mr. Eagan. The old man described him pretty clearly, besides, Mr. Eagan had just told us that himself. Then about four-thirty there was a woman. She was wearing a red raincoat with the hood up over her head. Then at five-fifteen there was another woman. But by then the light was failing and he couldn't see much, so he can't describe her to any extent, except just to say that she had on a brownish-coloured raincoat."

"And that's all?" Justin asked.

"That's all, I'm afraid."

"Have you told it all to Mrs. Thaine?"

"Yes. She says she has no idea who either woman could be. She doesn't know anyone with a red raincoat. She didn't think that her husband was expecting anybody."

"Well, naturally I can't help you," Justin said. "I don't know anyone in this neighbourhood but Mrs. DeLong." He turned to her. "You've really no idea about either of these women, Grace? None?"

"No," she said, "none at all."

"And," Turkis said, "you've no idea——" He hesitated, dropping his eyes to gaze reflectively into the sparking fire. "You've no idea, for instance, if by any chance Mr. Thaine would often have visits from women on Saturdays, when his wife was away in Wallport?"

"No, I've no idea," Grace said. "But I don't think so. No, I really don't think so." She paused, watching Turkis as he continued to stare at the fire in apparent embarrassment. That embarrassment worried Justin, for he was sure it was not in the least real. Grace went on, "I know how mistaken one can be about these things, but I don't think Arnold ever looked at any woman but Hester."

"And you've no idea what sort of reason might have taken either of those women there?" Turkis asked.

"Inspector, though I was a near neighbour of the Thaines and though I knew them both pretty well, I don't pretend to know everything there is to know about either of them." Grace's voice grated a little. "Arnold Thaine was a well-known man. He knew a great many people. I don't suppose he ever mentioned more than a quarter of them to me."

Turkis nodded calmly.

"That would be so, of course. And neither of those women was you, by any chance, Mrs. DeLong?"

It slid out casually. At the same moment, Turkis raised his eyes to her face.

He could not have missed the way her breath caught.

"I told you, it was in the morning that I went there," she said.

"Oh yes, so it was." Turkis nodded and stood up to go.

To Justin it seemed that there was something indescribably dangerous in the air just then. Turkis should not have accepted her answer with such readiness. He could not really have done so. Like his embarrassment, that acceptance was false.

As soon as the two detectives had gone, Justin told Grace what he thought of her.

"Let me tell you, if you want to lie," he said, "you've got to do better than that. Turkis came here for just one reason and that was to ask you that last question. And the only possible answer was the truth or else a round, definite 'No!' But you hesitated. Then you prevaricated. Now he knows two things for certain, that you did go to the Thaines' house in the afternoon and that you're lying about it. Good God, Grace, what's happened to you? You used not to be a fool."

Grace bent to pile some more coal on the fire.

"He's got no proof," she said.

"Don't be too sure."

"What proof could he have?"

"I don't know. But he's a deep one."

"He doesn't strike me that way. And if he's got a proof —which I'm sure he couldn't have—why didn't he accuse me of lying straight away?"

"Ever heard of giving a person enough rope to hang himself?"

He made it deliberately cruel, partly to shock some sense into her and partly to alleviate his own fear on her account. But as soon as he saw her face, he wished that he had spoken differently.

"Look, Grace," he went on urgently, "you told me yourself that you were at the Thaines' house in the afternoon. That means that up to a point you trust me. Well, why not go the rest of the way? Tell me why you lied to Turkis. Tell me the real reason why you went there."

" It wasn't to do murder."

" I know that."

" Do you, I wonder ? "

He held on to his temper with difficulty.

" Let's say that I do," he said, " and let's say too that I know as well as you do that you were the woman in the brown coat who went into the Thaines' house at five-fifteen——"

" But do either of us know that for certain ? " she interrupted.

He stared at her.

She went on, " Suppose I were to tell you that I went to the Thaines' house a good deal later than five-fifteen. Suppose I were to point out that a great many people have brown raincoats. But why bother ? It's for the police to find out who she was. And you've had no breakfast yet. Come along to the kitchen. I'd just made some coffee when those men turned up."

She went out.

Justin lit a cigarette before he followed her. His temper was now so raw that he was afraid of more argument. He felt as angry as a person who sees a child, too far off to be reached in time and refusing to listen to warning shouts, walk out into the traffic.

When, a few minutes later, he went out to the kitchen, he said as soon as he entered it, " How about dropping me at my hotel after breakfast ? "

" If you like," she answered.

" Or I can take a bus."

" No, I'll take you," she said.

They both spoke sullenly, both of them almost equally on edge.

She put a coffee-pot on the table. It was good coffee that she had made, very strong and black. They sat down, facing one another.

Justin intended to say no more about the murder. Indeed, he intended to say as little as possible and to leave as soon as he could. It should have been easy, for Grace seemed to have no desire to talk to him. She sat with her head resting on one hand and her unfocused stare going past him to the window. This morning it framed a square of pale blue sky, glittering with wintry sunshine. But in spite of Justin's resolution and almost before he realised that he was going to put the thought into words, he presently struck the table with his fist and exclaimed, " That dog ! "

Grace started and for an instant looked desperate and scared.

He went on, " It was shut up inside the house when Hester Thaine got there in the evening. Well, was it there when you were in the house ? "

" I don't know," Grace said.

" You couldn't help knowing. If it was there, it would have barked the house down when it heard you. If it didn't bark, it wasn't there."

" I didn't hear it," she said.

" That means then," he said with heavy sarcasm, " that besides Eagan, the woman in red, the hypothetical woman in brown and yourself, still another person went to the Thaines' house yesterday afternoon and let the dog in before Hester Thaine got back from Wallport."

" Not necessarily," Grace said.

" No, if you're lying again," he agreed.

" Or if Hester is."

He pushed his chair back from the table.

" What would be the purpose of that lie ? " he asked.

" Your guess is as good as mine."

" In other words, you don't really believe in what you've just suggested."

She shrugged her shoulders.

" I think I'm inclined to believe that the dog *was* in the house when you went there," Justin said. " I'm also rather inclined to believe that Thaine was in the house—alive or dead."

She set her cup down in its saucer with a bang. " And what else ? "

" I'm just thinking it out," he said. " You see, Thaine was in the house when Eagan went there at half-past three. Eagan says so. And the old man in the cottage never saw

Thaine leave. So presumably he was still there—alive or dead—when the woman in red called. And he was still there when you called——"

"When the woman in brown called. But when she left, it was already getting dark, remember. So if Arnold went out soon after that, the old man wouldn't have seen him either leave or return."

"So your theory is that Thaine left the house about five-thirty, that you arrived around six, when the house was empty and that Thaine returned after that, possibly plus murderer and dog."

"Well, what's wrong with that?"

"Just one thing. Thaine was killed sometime between three and five-thirty."

Her pale face seemed to turn a little greyer.

"I thought they couldn't be so accurate about that kind of thing," she said.

"Not between narrow limits, I believe. But two hours is a goodish time."

Grace's chair scraped noisily on the kitchen floor as she stood up.

"What are you trying to do, Justin? Convince yourself that I must have murdered Arnold?"

"Convince you that Turkis believes you're the woman in brown and that the wisest thing you can do is admit it and tell him the whole truth about your visit."

"The truth, the truth—you keep talking about the truth!" She went to the window and stood with her back to him. "D'you think I know what the truth is? I've been at sea for weeks, not understanding what was happening. I knew something was happening. I knew there was scheming going on and lying and deception. But I couldn't make any sense of it. I couldn't see any point in it. All I do know is, Brillhart's behind it. I don't know what he's been doing or what he wants, but I do know that he's to blame for the stories that are going round and that some people, I suppose, are beginning to believe. That's to say . . ." Her voice faltered.

Justin, who had turned in his chair and was watching her

intently, saw her lean her forehead against the window-pane as if she needed its coolness to relieve a pain.

" It has to be Brillhart," she muttered.

" What stories, Grace ? " Justin asked.

" Stories about Arnold and his work, for one thing," she said. " That he wasn't genuine. That he only cared about his old clocks and that his only real ability lay in picking on brilliant young men to do his work for him and getting rid of them and ruining them when they began to catch on to how he was using them. Fantastic, impossible, detestable stories."

" Yet the fact is," Justin said thoughtfully, " you half-believe them yourself."

" No ! "

He stood up. His body felt as stiff and tired as it would have if he had had to do quite without sleep.

" Well, suppose we get going," he said. " I'd like a shave and my things arc all at the hotel."

" All right," she said. " But—you aren't leaving, are you ? You aren't going back to London ? "

" D'you want me to stay ? "

" Yes."

" Damned if I can see what use I am to you when you won't even tell me . . ." But he was tired of saying that and stopped.

" You're a great help to me," Grace said, with a sudden threat of tears in her voice.

" All right," he said quickly, " but let's get going."

She drove him to his hotel. The morning was a fine one, far colder than the day before but with a pale wash of sunshine lying over the sodden ground. When Grace had driven off again, Justin went to his room and shaved. Afterwards, he lay on his bed for a while, smoking and trying to sort out some of his thoughts, mostly those of Grace, of her lies and her motives for lying. He realised that he had always thought of her as an extremely truthful person, yet really he did not know why. She had the kind of abruptness which it is easy to associate with candour and he could not remember ever having detected her in a lie of any importance.

Yet that could have been because of his own denseness, his lack of suspicion. It is always simplest to believe what other people say until they have been shown up, beyond all reasonable doubt, as liars, and the process of accepting the changed viewpoint is always painful. So it was possible that, over the years, Grace had deceived him over one thing and another, again and again.

Suddenly he realised that he was cold. There was an electric fire in the room, but the meter needed a shilling before he could switch it on. Feeling through his pockets, he found that he did not possess a single one. At that point, he decided to go out, acquire a supply of shillings and buy a newspaper.

He had not reached the newsagent's shop, which he had noticed on the far side of the square, when he heard his name called and Lewis Brillhart, with his dog at his heels, came hurrying up to him.

There was a good deal of excitement in Brillhart's manner and an emotional gleam in his protuberant eyes.

"Emery," he said, "I'm glad I saw you. I've been wanting to talk to you, but I didn't know where to find you. I could have telephoned Grace, of course, but you saw how she is about me. So this is a piece of luck. Come along to my house, won't you? It's only just along here."

He had the look of a person who is bursting with information which he cannot bear to keep to himself.

Quite glad to have someone to talk to, Justin let himself be led along. The dog trotted close behind him, his head lowered as if he were ready at any moment to take a bite at Justin's heels.

Brillhart lived in a small, terrace house with its frontage straight on to the street. It had probably been bought very cheaply, but a clever hand had altered and redecorated the small rooms, which were furnished with a skilful blending of the old and the new, and were uncommonly attractive.

Brillhart took Justin into a room that overlooked what would have been a commonplace backyard but that the walls had been white-washed, a rose trained up one of them and some small trees in tubs placed in the corners.

Seeing Justin looking out over the little yard, Brillhart came to his side, smiling.

"It isn't bad, is it?" he said. "When I bought the house—and I bought it, believe it or not, for only seven hundred—it was all just dustbins and the neighbours' cats. I've improved it, don't you think? In spring there are crocuses between the paving-stones. And d'you know, I picked a rose there only last week?" He brought some bottles of beer out of a cupboard. "I like to do that sort of thing," he added.

"D'you live here by yourself?" Justin asked. It struck him that, away from the shadow of Grace's sharp enmity, Brillhart had a far more agreeable personality than he had realised. There was a simplicity about it, something direct and unguarded that appealed to Justin.

"Oh yes, quite by myself," Brillhart said. "My wife is —well, she's been in hospital for rather a long time. So I do everything about the place. I like to. Particularly I like the cooking. You must come and eat with me one evening. You'll find I'm pretty good. By the way, how long are you staying?"

"That depends," Justin said.

"I see. Of course. Well, I'm glad you're here, because Grace needs someone to stop her acting foolishly. You've known her a long time, haven't you?"

"A pretty long time," Justin agreed.

"I think I've heard her speak of you—in the days when we were on speaking terms. Tell me, Emery, have you ever had a person whom you sincerely liked and admired suddenly turn against you for no reason that you've ever been able to discover?"

"I don't think I have," Justin said. "I've usually known the reasons only too well."

"Well, perhaps I'm not being quite honest," Brillhart said. "Perhaps I do know the reasons, or at least I can think of a reason which may or may not be the right one. But it's a rather stupid one, so I'm a little reluctant to believe in it, because Grace isn't usually stupid. She's a gifted, warm-hearted woman—not that she's ever made anything of her gifts, but she's got them—and I believe I respect her as much as anyone I've ever met. Certainly she helped me more than anyone else ever has, and I don't think I could ever forget that, however much her attitude to me changed. When I first met her, I was nearly desperate. . . . But that isn't what I meant to talk about. I wanted to ask you if you can't stop her lying to the police."

Justin drank some of the beer that Brillhart had given him, then looked curiously at the other man.

" Has she been lying to the police ? " he asked.

Brillhart considered him for a moment, without speaking, then smiled.

" As I said, I'm glad you're staying," he said. " Yes, Emery, she has. She denies having been to the Thaines' house in the afternoon. Yet she was seen going into it about five-fifteen by an old man in a cottage nearby. But perhaps you've heard all that."

" About the man and the two women ? "

" About Ben Eagan, Grace and some mysterious woman in red."

" What makes you say it was Grace ? " Justin asked.

Sitting down, Brillhart held his beer glass in his hands between his knees. He went on smiling.

" Of course it was Grace," he said, " She's always popping in there to keep an eye on Hester. Poor Grace, she thinks people haven't realised what's the matter with her. But perhaps they haven't. They don't know her as well as I do. I find her one of the most transparent people I've ever known. That's partly why I like her so much, even though she doesn't like me. I'm hoping she'll get over that some day—perhaps if she realises that it's not so terrible if I know her secret. What d'you think ? Has she said anything about it ? "

" I'm afraid I don't know what you're talking about," Justin said. " I don't know of any secret of hers and I don't know why she should try to keep an eye on Mrs. Thaine."

" Don't you ? Don't you really ? Oh well, if that's so . . ." Brillhart looked as if this had given him something new to think about.

"What are your theories about Thaine's murder?" Justin asked.

"Oh, I haven't any theories yet. Not to take seriously. And if it weren't for that visit of Grace's . . ."

"Well?"

"I'd say a burglar, of course. Yet it seems that nothing was taken."

"So you don't believe in the burglar?"

"Well, do you?"

"I know so little about the circumstances," Justin said. "About Thaine, I mean, and his relations with the people around him."

"No, and even if you knew as much as I do, you'd be uncertain. . . . Take Grace's visit, for instance. If the police are right about the time of the murder, then Thaine must have been dead already when she was there. That's supposing that she didn't kill him herself. I prefer to suppose that, though when it comes to violence . . . However, that's nothing to go by. We're all violent inside, I suppose. But the point is, I know of only one person whom Grace would lie to protect. And what I'd like to know is, has she any actual knowledge about that person, or is she just torturing herself unnecessarily with some unfounded suspicion and getting herself into a dangerous situation in the process? If that's so . . ."

Justin found that he was beginning to dislike Brillhart's unfinished sentences. They managed to suggest too many things.

"I told you," he said, "I know so little of the situation, I can't offer an opinion."

"Well, think it out, then," Brillhart said. "The really important thing is to identify the woman in red, isn't it?"

"D'you know who she was?"

"No, nor does anyone else, apparently."

"You're suggesting she did the murder?"

"Not necessarily. But if there was some woman in Arnold's life of whom we all know nothing . . ." Again the sentence went unfinished. Brillhart drank up the rest of his beer. "It's easier to pin your suspicions on an unknown person than on someone you know," he added, half-apologetically. "But actually it surprises me that there was someone. . . . I'd have sworn that Arnold wasn't really much interested in women and I know he set a great value on Hester. I wouldn't say he exactly loved her, or gave her much of what a man normally gives a woman— I've always been rather sorry for her, you know, she deserved something better than she got. But still, he prized her, he admired her. There wasn't much warmth in him, he hadn't much capacity for affection, except perhaps for all those clocks of his, but still, he recognised something rare and fine when he found it and he handled it accordingly. It would really amaze me unspeakably to learn that he was unfaithful to Hester."

Though his words were so measured, Brillhart's face, while he was speaking of Hester Thaine, took on almost the same expression as it had worn the evening before, when he had gone to meet her across the room.

"So what *is* your opinion about the woman in red ? " Justin asked.

"Only that it's important to find her."

"There I agree with you."

"Her errand may or may not have been an important one, but at least she knows whether or not Arnold was dead already when she went in, and that should be important for Grace."

"If he was dead, she's taking her time coming forward to say so."

"Just so, which suggests guilt of some sort."

"But if he wasn't dead ? "

"If she says that he wasn't and if she can convince the police that she's telling them the truth, then the outlook for Grace may be very unpleasant. You do see that, don't you, Emery ? That's really why I wanted to have this talk with you. You're a friend of hers, you're in her confidence. Once that woman in the red coat has been found, Grace's situation may become critical. It's essential that she should understand that."

"The woman in the red coat . . ."

For some reason, the phrase affected Justin strangely. It changed his image of the unknown woman. Until that moment, he had been visualising her as a figure in a dark red, dripping raincoat, hurrying furtively through the downpour. Now suddenly he saw her dressed in vivid scarlet, with sunshine falling on her bright, fair hair. A youthful figure, stepping down from a bus, standing in his way for a moment.

"Good God," he exclaimed softly, "could that be . . . ?"
Instantly excited by his tone, Brillhart sprang up.
"What is it? What have you thought of?"
"It's nothing—just an idea. Tell me, Brillhart, those buses that go to Fallow Corner from the square here—where do they come from?"
"From Wallport. Why?"
"Just an idea," Justin repeated. "There's no reason to think there's anything in it."
All the same, as soon after that as he was able, he took his leave of Brillhart, crossed the square to a public telephone, dialled the number of the police station and asked for Inspector Turkis.

VII

Turkis, Justin was told, was at the Thaines' house. He took a taxi and went there at once. He did not allow himself to wonder how foolish his excitement might appear to Turkis, or to consider how many women altogether might have been seen the day before in Archersfield wearing red coats. The point about the woman whom Justin himself had seen was that she had come on the bus from Wallport. She brought in a foreign element, one that might lead anywhere and at least draw suspicion away from Fallow Corner.

When he reached the house, Hester Thaine opened the door to him. Behind her in the hall stood Turkis, who appeared just to be leaving.

Hester was now dressed in black, a severely cut, close-fitting dress without any touch of colour yet which entirely lacked the look of mourning. It clung too closely to her slender figure, emphasising the fragile elegance that had impressed Justin the evening before. Her face was extremely pale and her eyes were red-veined with weariness.

Justin apologised for thrusting himself on her again, then told her and Turkis of the girl in the red coat.

Turkis, in his detached fashion, seemed to be interested, said he would look into the matter, then left. Justin would have left with him but that Hester stopped him.

" I'm glad you came," she said, as she closed the door behind Turkis. " I was hoping to see you. There's something—something I want somebody to do for me and I'd already thought of asking you—as a matter of fact, I was just going to telephone Grace to ask if I could speak to you when the inspector came—but it's better like this. If you don't mind, that is."

She spoke breathlessly, as if she were in a far more nervous state than the pallid and expressionless composure of her face suggested.

Following her into the drawing-room, Justin remembered that she was under the impression that he was staying with Grace. The thought rather annoyed him ; however, he said nothing just then to correct Hester's mistake.

He noticed that the room had an uncared-for look. There was a film of dust on the furniture and there were cigarette-ends in the ash-trays. A great many cigarette-ends. They had not been there the evening before. Brillhart had stayed late, then.

" What can I do ? " Justin asked her.

" You won't mind my asking you ? "

" How could I ? "

" But if you don't want to do what I ask . . ."

" I think I'll want to do it."

She smiled uncertainly. She was very tense.

" Then sit down and stay and talk for a little," she said, " because I don't think I'll be able to ask you straight out without some explanation. It's something in a way very personal and we're strangers. Yet when I thought of it, it was you I thought of asking at once to do it. But that's hardly fair on you, is it? You may find it an awkward and embarrassing thing to do, seeing that you hardly know us here. But that's partly why I thought of you—that you don't know us. You won't be suspected of prejudice."

"Then it has nothing to do with Grace," he said, "this thing that you want me to do? Because, where she's concerned, perhaps I have prejudices."

"No, it has nothing to do with Grace. That is—no." She frowned. "Please sit down," she repeated.

He did not want to sit down. He was too restless and too tense himself. But he dropped into one of the velvet-covered chairs.

She was silent then, looking as if she had forgotten what she had meant to say to him. When her next remark came, it was as if she were making it to herself, rather than to him.

"I wonder how much you know about us all by now," she said.

When he did not answer she went on, "This girl in the red coat now—if she was the one who came here—I know nothing about her at all. I'm not sure if the police believe that, but of course Arnold had all sorts of connections I knew nothing about, business connections and so on. And old friends. I never mixed much with his friends. Our marriage was really a very private sort of thing, set apart from the rest of our lives. That was how I liked it. I'm naturally a rather solitary sort of person and people wear me out very quickly, but Arnold had enormous vitality and liked to talk by the hour, usually stirring people up into arguments that excited and exhilarated him immensely. I never enjoyed that sort of thing. So I kept out of it when I could and so naturally I don't know much about the people. . . . This isn't what I was meaning to say to you."

Justin still kept silence. He had been shaken by the unhappiness behind her words, which he felt sure she was unaware of having betrayed to him. He did not think that she had had any intention of portraying herself as a lonely woman, casually neglected by her dominating husband, deeply bewildered by her marriage and perhaps close to a sense of complete inner defeat.

Hester watched him questioningly for a moment, then went on, " I'm sorry, I know it would be better if I went straight to the point, but I find it so difficult. It's about Ben Eagan and his visits here yesterday."

Standing up again, Justin began to fiddle with an ornament on the mantelpiece. All at once he felt very afraid of saying the wrong thing to her, of revealing an understanding to her that might actually do her some degree of harm. His silence, which until then had been unthinking, became deliberate, almost determined.

" You see," she said, " I'd like to know—I want to know—his reasons for coming."

Justin looked closely at the ornament, then pushed it away from him.

"Have you seen him to-day ? " he asked.

"Yes, he came over early this morning."

" Didn't he tell you his reasons ? "

" He told me—but you see, I don't believe him—he told me it was to ask Arnold to mend his watch for him."

" Why don't you believe him ? "

" Oh, I don't mean I don't believe he did ask Arnold to mend his watch. But I think he had some other reason as well for coming."

" And you want me to find out what it was ? "

A flush mounted in her cheeks. " Not that, exactly. That is, you could handle it how you liked, of course. But if you could persuade him to tell *me* what really happened. . . . You see, I know he and Arnold had a violent quarrel the evening before. It was in our village pub and a lot of people heard it. So it'd be no use pretending it didn't happen, would it ? And it seems to me that people are sure to start saying that his visits yesterday had something to do with it. So if only he would tell me what it was all really about . . ."

" The quarrel ? "

" That, for one thing."

" You didn't hear it yourself, then ? "

" No, I wasn't there."

" How did you hear of it ? "

She shrank a little from the question.

" A woman I met in Wallport market yesterday told me
about it," she said. " She told me as if it were a joke and
swore she hadn't heard what it was all about. Well, till I
got home, I didn't think much about it. If Arnold got
excited in an argument, you might easily think he was
quarrelling, when in fact he was only enjoying himself. He
and Ben often argued madly about the most ridiculous
things, looking as if they might be at one another's throats
at any minute. Then Arnold would come home and say
that he'd had a really good evening and praise Ben for
having such a good mind and being able to stick up for
himself. Only I don't think many people understood that,
and now that this—this thing has happened, I'm afraid that
they're going to start remembering that quarrel in the pub
and enlarging on it and saying that, after a quarrel like that,
it's absurd to suppose that Ben would come here to ask
Arnold to mend his watch for him. So I would like Ben to
tell me the truth about it all—the quarrel and his visits here
—so that . . ." Her voice, which had been growing hoarse,
dried up at that point.

" So that you know how to defend him if people suggest
that he murdered your husband ? " Justin said.

She coughed once or twice, trying to clear her throat.

" So that at least I know what to think myself," she said.

Justin thrust his fidgeting hands into his pockets.

" Mrs. Thaine, are you afraid that Ben Eagan murdered
your husband ? "

" Oh no," she said.

He sighed. It was what they all said, he thought, when
you asked them a straight question. Oh no.

" Then what exactly have you to fear ? " he asked.

She did not answer. From the blankness of her face, it
did not look as if she were even trying to answer.

After a moment Justin went on, " I'll try to help you in
any way I can——"

" I know you will," she put in.

" —so why not tell me what you're really afraid of ? "

" I don't really know," she said, " but I've been afraid
for some time. You see, there have been stories going
around. . . ." She stopped again and a look of intense
reluctance to say any more appeared on her face.

" I believe I've heard some mention of stories," Justin
said.

In a suddenly violent tone, she exclaimed, " I believe it's
one of the easiest things in the world to spread a slander !
These stories—they're that Arnold wasn't a genuine artist,
that he was a fake who knew how to exploit the abilities of
the young men who came to learn from him, that he took
their designs and adapted them a little bit and put his own
name on them. You wouldn't really believe it was possible
to spread such stories, would you ? But people like to
believe evil of one another——"

" Wait a minute," Justin said. " Let me get this clear.
This thing that you're afraid of . . . Are you afraid that
Eagan spread this slander ? "

" No ! "

" But who else would benefit by it ? "

" I don't know. I don't think anyone would benefit."

" It was something entirely irrational, then ? "

" What else could it have been ? But listen——" A
nervous animation came into her manner. " Suppose those
stories had finally got round to Arnold. I always hoped they
wouldn't, but such things usually happen sooner or later.
And suppose, like you, he jumped to the conclusion that
Ben must have spread the stories and accused him of it—
accused him in the pub, where everyone heard it . . . If it
happened like that, no one could believe that Ben would
come here next day and ask Arnold to mend his watch for
him, could they ? "

" Have you some reason for believing that that *was* what
happened in the pub ? " Justin asked.

" Well, in a way."

" Who told you about it, then ? Someone must have told
you about it *after* you'd talked with the woman in the
market. Was it Brillhart ? "

She nodded.

"Last night, after Grace and I had gone?" Justin asked.

"Only he didn't tell me about it at all," she said. "He wouldn't. But he got so embarrassed when I tried to make him tell me that I can't think of any other explanation."

"Well, I'll see what I can do," Justin said, speaking out of a deep reluctance. "But you realise that it would be quite natural in Eagan to tell me to mind my own business?"

"I don't think he will. Ben's very nice. He'll understand that you're trying to help."

"I wonder. . . . However, I'll go straight away and when I've seen him, I'll telephone you to tell you how it went."

She thanked him with a vivid smile. But immediately afterwards her face grew absent-minded and Justin felt that as soon as her end had been gained, she had almost forgotten that he was still in the room with her.

He walked to Eagan's cottage. The day was no longer so fine and a dark patch of cloud, growing larger in the west, suggested that there might be rain again later on. As he walked, Justin wondered if there was any chance that Eagan might not be in. Justin was full of pity for Hester, anxious to help her and rather attracted by her, but if something quite outside himself, such as the absence of Eagan, had prevented his complying with the demand that she had made on him he would have been profoundly thankful.

Eagan, however, was in. He came to the door, holding a chunk of bread and cheese in one hand and showing no surprise at seeing Justin. He seemed, if anything, to be glad that he had come. Inviting Justin to join him in bread and cheese and beer, Eagan let him into the small, dirty kitchen, again muttering apologies for its condition.

"I suppose Grace is quite right, I'm no good at managing on my own," he said as he washed a plate under the tap. "The only thing is, it doesn't worry me. You can't get some people to understand that."

His eyes were ringed with shadow, but his manner was oddly unconcerned. He dried the plate and set it down on the table, then started to wash a glass.

"Have you seen Grace this morning?" he asked.

"Yes—and Mrs. Thaine," Justin said. "She told me you'd been to see her."

"Yes, I went round early this morning. Well, not so early, really. Last night, after you'd gone, I started being sick and it went on most of the night. That's the way I act in a crisis. It makes me thoroughly ashamed of myself, but that doesn't seem to stop it. Anyway, I didn't want to see Hester till I'd got over making a fool of myself." He put the glass down before Justin and filled it with beer. "I saw that policeman too and heard about the two women who'd been seen going into the house. Personally, I don't think either of them had anything to do with it."

Justin was feeling pleased with his diagnosis of character. "Why not?" he asked.

"Arnold was pretty careful to keep clear of women," Eagan said. "I think the motive for his murder was theft."

"But if nothing was taken?"

"Who knows that nothing was taken? Who could tell for certain if a clock was missing? And some of those clocks are pretty valuable."

"Wouldn't Mrs. Thaine know that?"

"I doubt it. She hated that room and never went into it, if she could help it. I don't blame her either. It did queer things to me when I went in."

"I understand that." Biting into some bread and cheese, Justin discovered all of a sudden that he was extremely hungry. "Can you explain Thaine's mania for clocks in any way?"

"I suppose it's just the same as any other sort of collecting."

"But that he should have made no attempt to get them to keep time . . ."

Eagan gave his smile of great charm, the tentative, half-apologetic smile that Justin had noticed the evening before.

"I've got a theory about that. Don't take me too seriously, but the fact is, I believe that Arnold had an idea that it would be wrong of him to impose his own will on them."

He was able to speak Thaine's name, Justin noticed,

without any noticeable heightening of emotion. His night of sickness seemed to have left him extraordinarily calm.

Eagan went on, " Sounds cock-eyed, doesn't it ? But I really believe he felt something like that, all the more because, in handling people, it never occurred to him to do anything but impose his will on them. But he half-realised, all the same, that you don't really get the best out of people if you simply make them tick in the same way as you do yourself. So he let the clocks have their freedom."

" A kind of atonement ? "

Eagan gave his diffident smile. " I told you not to take me too seriously."

" It's as good a theory as any I can think of," Justin said. " But talking of the two women who went into the house, didn't the police tell you that you'd been seen there yourself?"

" Oh yes," Eagan said unconcernedly. " I told them myself I'd been there."

" And why you went ? "

" Yes, to ask Arnold to mend my watch. If I'd taken it to a man in Archersfield, he'd have kept it for weeks and probably mucked it up while he was at it. But Arnold did that sort of thing beautifully."

Again Justin noticed the detachment with which he spoke of Thaine, almost as if he had already been dead for a long time.

Helping himself to more bread, Justin said, " I came here this morning with a message about your watch from Mrs. Thaine, and about what you told the police. I'm sorry—I don't like pushing myself into your affairs—but this is what she wanted me to say . . ."

He became aware, as he was speaking, that Eagan had suddenly become very still.

Deliberately avoiding looking at him, spreading butter on his bread with great concentration, Justin went on, " She wanted me to tell you that various people heard you and Thaine quarrelling in the pub on the evening before his murder, and that when the police are told about that, they aren't going to believe that you went over to his house next day to ask him to mend your watch. She wants you to face that and to tell her why you really went there, so that the two of you can think out the best thing to do—because you realise, don't you, that if the police succeed in tracking the woman with the red coat and if she should claim, truthfully or not, that Thaine was already dead when she went into the house, your position could be very serious ? " He paused, bit off some bread and cheese, then repeated uncomfortably round the mouthful, " Sorry—I know it's not my business."

Eagan made no movement and for a moment did not answer, then he said rather wonderingly, " Hester said that, did she ? Does she think I murdered her husband ? "

" I'm not really quite sure," Justin said.

" Who told her about that quarrel ? "

" A woman she met in Wallport. Then she questioned Brillhart about it, but he wouldn't say anything."

" Does she know what it was about ? "

" She thinks it was because Thaine suspected you of spreading slanderous stories about him."

Eagan's eyebrows shot up. " Slanderous stories about *him* ? "

Justin said nothing.

Eagan explained, " I've run across a slanderous story about myself and it was that that we quarrelled about. Arnold had heard it too and believed it. That's to say, when he'd had a few drinks he believed it, or pretended that he did, for the sake of the argument. That's to say . . ." A look of confusion clouded his dark eyes. " That's what I thought at the time. And now that I've admitted that much, I may as well tell you the rest——"

" You don't have to," Justin said.

" I know. All the same . . . You see, next morning I couldn't make up my mind whether or not he'd been serious the night before. So I thought I'd better go and find out, because if he had been, there was only one thing I could do. But my watch had stopped and so had this clock here, so actually I hadn't the faintest idea what the time was when I went there. Well, when I got to the Thaines' house, I found no one about and when I looked into the studio from the window I saw that the fire hadn't even been lit. It was just a lot of ashes from the night before. I remember a clock on the wall said it was ten minutes to eight. Of course, that didn't mean anything; still, I decided I must have turned up at some fantastically early hour and that no one was up yet. So I went home. On the way I met Grace and she told me what the time really was and it wasn't so very early. Still, I left it for the time being, but later on I tried again and that time I found Arnold in the studio. As I'd more or less expected, he was perfectly friendly, apologised for some of the things he'd said the night before, told me that he'd got other worries on his mind and that that was why he'd talked so absurdly, and the end of it was that I asked him if he'd mend my watch for me and he said he'd be delighted. So there you are. I don't know whether or not it sounds convincing to you, but it's what happened."

" Will you tell it all to Mrs. Thaine ? " Justin asked.

" Couldn't you ? "

" Is that what you want me to do ? "

" I think so. If you would."

" But I can't tell her anything about the cause of the quarrel."

" No," Eagan agreed.

" So that's why you want to leave the job to me—simply because I shan't be able to answer her questions."

" Well . . . it would be a help."

Justin tilted his chair back, looking up meditatively at the kitchen ceiling. Then he reached for his glass, drained it, set it down again and stood up.

" I think I'll keep out of it," he said. " You do what you think best about it."

Anxiety showed at once on Eagan's face. " But couldn't you possibly . . . ? "

" I came with a message," Justin said. " But I don't want to get deep into a situation I don't understand. I imagine you can see my point of view."

" Yes, I can see it, of course," Eagan said. " Well, I'll think it over. Perhaps I'll go over presently and tell her the whole thing myself. Anyway, thanks for coming."

He got up and went to the door with Justin.

Justin walked towards Grace's house. He was not thinking precisely of what he should do next, but her house was there, only a short way down the road. If a bus had not come by then, and stopped a few yards ahead of him, he would probably have gone in to see Grace and discussed with her his conversations with Eagan, Hester and Brillhart. But the bus appearing at that moment, he sprinted the few yards to catch it.

Sitting inside it, he found himself thinking about that half-written letter that he had seen the evening before on Eagan's table. It had been a letter to Thaine and contained Eagan's resignation from his job with him. That hardly squared with what Eagan had just told Justin of his interview with Thaine, the friendly interview, all goodwill and apologies. Justin grimaced. Then he told himself that it was not his business. But the trouble was that he was not wholly convinced of that. He was somehow already involved with these people and the question of what was his business and what was not had become as many-sided as any other question of human relations.

When he arrived in Archersfield and got off the bus, he remembered that he had still no shillings for the meter in his room and that he had not yet bought a Sunday paper. Not very hopeful that the newsagent would still be open, he started across the square towards the shop.

Again something stopped him before he reached it.

Someone was standing in the doorway of the shop, barring his entrance. It was a girl, who was reading a newspaper. She was holding the paper opened out before her and was staring at some paragraph in it with a look of horrified amazement on her face. The coat she was wearing was of bright scarlet.

VIII

THINGS HAPPENED quickly then.

The girl suddenly crumpled the newspaper under one arm, ran across the square to the bus that Justin had left and jumped on to it.

Her flight took him by surprise. He had not had time to decide what to do about her, whether to speak to her, to fetch Turkis, or to follow her at a distance and find out for himself, if he could, what her business was in Archersfield.

She had glanced at him before she started to run, but had seemed unaware of him and of the fixity with which he was staring at her. Her vacant gaze, under brows contracted in an effort at thought, had gone through him and past him so dazedly that it seemed to him possible that she actually had not seen anyone standing there close to her.

She was not quite so young as Justin had remembered her in his sunlit vision, nor perhaps quite so pretty, though it might have been that the haggardness in her face had come there only at that moment, with the panic that had over-powered her as she read the newspaper. In spite of her fair hair her eyes were dark brown, almost black. It startled him to realise it.

The bus had just begun to move when Justin grabbed the rail and swung himself on to it.

As he did so, he heard his name shouted behind him.

For an instant he had to struggle to keep his feet on the platform of the moving bus, but when he looked over his shoulder, he saw Brillhart waving to him with one hand, while with the other he clutched the collar of his dog, which was straining to chase Justin and the bus. Brillhart was shouting, but, except for his own name, Justin could not make out what he was saying.

The bus began to gather speed and Justin, signalling to Brillhart that he could not hear him, stepped inside and sat down near the door. The girl in red was sitting at the front of the bus. She was sitting bolt upright, staring before her, her hands rustling the newspaper, though she did not look at it again.

By degrees, as the bus continued on its way, she relaxed a little, but so far as Justin could see, all the way to Wallport she never once looked down at the paper. Once or twice she looked behind her, as if she felt his scrutiny, and on one of those occasions her bright, dark eyes looked into his, but still without the signs of any particular awareness of him. However, after that, she fidgeted more than she had before, a great restlessness growing upon her as the bus drew near to the town.

The whole journey from Archersfield to the terminus in Wallport took three-quarters of an hour. But the girl did not go to the terminus. When the bus stopped at a crossing, which must be, Justin thought, very near to the end of the journey, she at first remained seated, so that it did not occur to Justin that she had any thought in her mind of moving; then, as the lights changed from red to orange, she rose swiftly and in spite of the conductor's warning, jumped off the bus and walked quickly away.

Though the bus was already moving and though the conductor tried to stop him, Justin managed to get off the bus and to set off after the girl. But he knew that this would make it obvious to her, if she was already suspicious, that he was following her.

That she was suspicious and that she had executed this manoeuvre on purpose to evade him, at first seemed to him certain. Yet as she walked off, she did not look back to find out whether or not she had been successful in leaving him behind. Hurrying straight to a telephone-box, she stepped inside. So perhaps, Justin thought, it had been simply the sight of the telephone-box near to the crossing, suddenly penetrating to her shocked mind, that had made her plunge from the bus.

When she came out of the telephone-box, she was no longer in a hurry. With her hands in her pockets and her head bent, she walked along slowly, looking as if she had nowhere in particular to go. Turning towards the sea-front she walked on slowly along the promenade. As if she had suddenly felt a chill coming in from the sea, she turned up the collar of her coat, but she did not look out into the grey distance or up at the gulls circling in the sky, but kept her gaze on the ground before her.

There were few other people on the promenade. The seats were deserted and on the pebbly beach the gulls pecked undisturbed amongst the seaweed. At one point, a flock of them wheeled noisily, quarrelling with each other over fragments of bread that an old woman, muffled up in scarves, was throwing to them. The sea itself was held in a steely calm, almost motionless.

Justin followed about twenty yards behind the girl. He was still not quite certain whether or not she knew that he was following her. Presently she sat down on one of the empty benches and, stretching her legs out before her, crossing one ankle over the other, leant back, keeping her hands dug deep in her pockets. She now turned her moody gaze on the sea.

Justin hesitated, then walked past her and sat down at the far end of the bench.

It was a minute before she turned her head towards him. He thought, when she did so, that she looked more puzzled than anything else, as if she had been unaware of him till then but now found herself thinking that perhaps she had seen him before. She seemed neither scared nor worried.

"You *are* following me, aren't you?" she said. "Why?"

"Why did you run away?" he countered.

She frowned, puzzled again. She was about twenty-six or twenty-seven, with a small, delicate face, pinched by the cold so that it seemed colourless, while the big dark eyes watched him thoughtfully from shadowy sockets. It was not at all the face that had left the vivid impression of brightness in Justin's memory. Yet it was easy to imagine it changing back to that brightness in a moment of excitement or warmth.

"Run away—from you?" she asked.

"From what you read in the paper," he answered.

"Are you a policeman, then?"

" No."

" Who are you ? " There was a slight childishness in her way of speaking. The caution in her tone was like that of a little girl who hesitates in giving her confidence to a stranger, not out of any suspicion of the stranger, but out of fear of breaking some half-comprehended rule of behaviour.

" I got taken calling on murder by a friend," Justin said. " But the police are looking for you. Do you know that ? "

" No, I—I didn't know. Of course I'm going to them. I ought to have gone at once, I suppose, as soon as I read that bit in the paper, but I just lost my head and then I saw the bus. . . . Will they understand that when I explain it to them, do you think, or will they think I really meant to run away ? "

Justin did not attempt to answer that question.

" Was that the first you knew of it, when you opened the paper ? " he asked.

A shudder ran through her.

" Yes. But why are the police looking for me ? How do they know about me ? "

That second question might have implied a number of different things and a careless answer, Justin recognised, would give away how little he knew about her.

" You were seen," he said.

" D'you mean, when I——" She stopped. At last a spark of suspicion glinted in the dark eyes. " How do *you* know about me ? "

" I saw you yesterday in Archersfield."

" At Arnold Thaine's house ? "

" No, in the town."

" But then I don't see . . ."

" Never mind about that, it's a long story," he said. " The main point is, you were at his house, weren't you, at about four-thirty ? "

" Yes. And I was going to see him again to-day, to ask him if he'd made up his mind about the clock. But then I saw the newspaper . . ."

" So you did see him yesterday ? "

He hoped he did not sound or look as tense as he felt

when he asked this question. If he did, the girl did not seem to notice it, or to understand what she had really been asked.

"Oh yes, he was very nice about my walking in like that," she said.

"Wasn't he expecting you?"

"Of course not. And I felt so awful about it too, when he explained my mistake. But he *was* nice. I think he had one of the most attractive personalities I've ever known." Saying it, she blushed girlishly. "That's why it was such a shock to-day. I mean, to think that only a little later . . . Because it can't have been much later, can it?"

"No." Justin's voice sounded muffled. It was no more than he had been expecting, yet to hear her say it and to imagine her repeating it to Turkis and to realise how directly her evidence would point his suspicions at Grace, brought down a weight like lead on Justin's spirits. "What was this mistake of yours?" he asked.

"Why, thinking that he kept a shop," she said.

"A furniture-shop? So he did, in a way."

"No, a clock-shop. I'd heard about his collection of clocks and I thought they were for sale. It was really an awful mistake to make."

"You mean you went there to buy a clock?"

She nodded her head vigorously.

"Yes, as a present for my grandmother. I live with her now, you see, and it's her eightieth birthday next week and I know she's very proud of it and rather excited and so I wanted to buy her something special. But at first I didn't have any good ideas about it. Then someone in the hotel told me about Arnold Thaine and his collection of clocks and I thought a really nice antique clock, the kind with cupids and painted flowers and so on, would be just the sort of thing that she'd love." She paused, looking troubled, as if she had felt suddenly that she was offering too much information on what were purely personal matters.

"Do you and your grandmother live in Wallport," Justin asked, "or are you here on a visit?"

"Oh, it's only a visit," she said. "We came down last week. We're staying at an hotel. I believe Granny's been spending the winter there for years, and she loves it, though actually it's rather dull. Still, I don't mind it. I go around sightseeing by myself a good deal and as it's the first chance I've had to see anything of England—my father worked in Bombay, you see, but he died last summer— there's plenty for me to do."

"I suppose so," Justin said. With entire futility, he was cursing himself for the impulse that had made him jump on the bus and follow the girl and listen to what she had to say. For everything that she said thrust Grace into sharper danger. If what the girl had just told him of herself was true, then, like himself, she had merely paid a call on murder, left her card behind and gone. She could, of course, be lying. Yet if she had spent all her life, except for the last few months, in India, how could she have become acquainted with Thaine?

"You said something about going to see Arnold Thaine to see if he'd made up his mind about a clock," Justin said. "Did you persuade him to sell you one after all?"

"Well, yes, I did, in a way," she said. "That is, when he'd explained my mistake to me and I'd apologised and was leaving as fast as I could, feeling dreadfully embarrassed, he stopped me and asked, supposing I could buy one of the clocks in the room, which one I would choose. So I pointed at one which was just like what I'd had in my mind and said, 'That one.' And Mr. Thaine laughed and said, 'All right, I'll think about it. Come back to-morrow and per- haps I'll let you have it.' I don't suppose he meant it really, but still, just on the chance, I was going back."

"It wasn't by any chance a clock over the mantelpiece that you pointed at, a lantern-clock?" Justin asked.

"No, it was on a shelf, I think," she said. "It was all china cupids and things, under a glass bell."

"D'you remember the clock over the mantelpiece?"

"Vaguely, I think."

"You don't remember the time it showed when you were in the room?"

"Oh no. I remember the time on the one with the cupids, though. It said a quarter to two."

" That doesn't help, I'm afraid."

He was glad that it did not help. One thing at least was missing from her story to damn Grace.

" Now tell me," she said, leaning a little towards him, " you *are* a policeman, aren't you ? "

" No, I'm not." But he felt that he owed her more than that. " I'm a friend of a friend of Arnold Thaine's. I've talked with the police, but that's all."

" That's how you knew about me, then ? " she said.

" More or less."

" But how do they know about me ?—Oh yes, you said I was seen. But that's rather frightening, you know. I mean, that they should find out about me so quickly. After all, in a little town like Archersfield, you hardly ever see a policeman. You'd hardly know they existed." Standing up, she stamped her feet once or twice, as if they had been growing cold while she sat on the bench. " I suppose I ought to go straight back there and tell them what I've told you."

Justin stood up beside her. " Yes, I think so."

" But first I'll have to go back to the hotel and explain things to Granny. I told her I'd be back by tea-time." She started to walk slowly along the promenade, but seemed to take it for granted that Justin would accompany her, for she went on talking. " I'll have to make a telephone call too. I tried to when I got off the bus, but I couldn't get through. It was to my fiancé, Kenneth Hersey, in London. . . . By the way, my name's Doris Allwood."

" Mine's Justin Emery."

" You see, I wanted to tell Kenneth the whole story quickly and ask him what I ought to do. For instance, ought I to tell Granny about it, or would it upset her too much at her age ? I'm still not really sure about that. What do you think ? Should I tell her what's happened, or should I make up some story about why I've got to go out ? "

" What kind of an old lady is she ? "

" Sharp as a needle. But her heart isn't very strong."

" If she's the kind of old lady who reads the newspapers and takes an interest in things, I think I'd tell her the whole story," Justin said. " She'll find out anyhow."

" Yes, so she will. Well, I'll do it straight away then—
unless——" She stood still, a speculative look coming into
her eyes. " Unless you'd come back with me and tell her
yourself. I think that would be a good idea."

" But I'm a complete stranger."

" Yes, that's why. You see, if I go in by myself and tell
her the story, she's rather likely to make up her own mind
what I ought to do about it. She's an autocratic old thing
with a very strong will and I may find that I'm ordered
straight back to London, or something, in an attempt to
keep me out of the scandal."

" But if you tell her that you've already been identified . . ."

" She may decide not to believe me. But if you tell her,
she'll believe you. Then we could go back to Archersfield
together and get it over."

" Well, if that's what you really want . . ."

But the request had startled him and like the girl herself,
disturbed him a good deal. The naïveté and the self-con-
fidence which made her apparently accept him with so little
suspicion and chatter to him with so little reserve would
have been more appropriate at seventeen than at twenty-
seven, or whatever her age was, and as they walked on
towards the hotel, Justin began to think that perhaps her
odd invitation had really not been given for the reason that
she had offered, but as a test of some sort ; that she had
devised some scheme for checking up on him, and that, in
fact, she was not nearly so naïve as she appeared.

The hotel to which she took him was one of the older and
less ostentatious hotels of Wallport, facing the promenade.
It was also one of the most expensive hotels in the town.
Old-fashioned comfort, the costliest thing in the world,
was the effect it aimed at.

Mrs. Allwood had a private sitting-room on the first floor.
She was a short, monolithic old lady, who looked immov-
ably planted in a chair by the fire. Her small, fat feet, in
beaded slippers, were on a crimson footstool, her square
head, with the grey hair cropped short like a man's, seemed
to jut up only a trifle above the solid mass of her shoulders.
She was tightly encased, from head to foot, in a green and

red plaid. She had her granddaughter's dark, bright eyes, though one was filmed with cataract. Nothing about her stirred, as she listened to the story that the girl told her.

When the girl finished, the old lady turned her head a little and looked steadily and thoughtfully at Justin.

Then she said, " Please ring the bell, Mr. Emery. I think we'll have tea."

While he was looking round for the bell, she went on, " Next time you pay calls, Doris, on men who are likely to get murdered, don't wear that red coat of yours. It catches the eye quite inescapably."

Doris laughed, with a trace of hysteria in her voice.

" Is that how I was spotted, Mr. Emery ? " she asked. " Was it just the red coat ? "

" Mostly," he admitted.

She unbuttoned the coat hurriedly. But then, instead of taking it off, she fidgeted with it for a moment and began to button it again.

" We'll be going out in a few minutes," she muttered. " But first I want to ring up Kenneth."

" You'll have tea before you go out again," her grand-mother said. " The police can wait just that little extra while."

" All right," Doris said. " But I must talk to Kenneth first."

She went out.

" And now, Mr. Emery," Mrs. Allwood said, " I am going to make a telephone call, too. Please hand me that instrument."

There was one on a small table not really out of her reach, but she made no motion towards it. Justin moved the small table to her side.

" Don't go," she went on. " This is not private."

Her call was to the police station in Archersfield. She was brief and businesslike. When she put the telephone down again, she said, " It appears that you are the person whom you claim to be, so I will allow my granddaughter to return with you. She must, of course, go to the police and answer any questions they put to her. But it's a most unfortunate

thing that she should have got herself involved in this
unsavoury affair. She's really quite a stranger in this
country. She was born in India and lived there until her
father died—he was an engineer in Bombay—and like many
girls growing up in the East, she has really led a very
sheltered sort of existence. I often find her notions concerning people and their behaviour in a sense quite old-
fashioned. I do not exaggerate when I say that there are
moments when I feel that I belong to the modern world
and she to the one that I remember as a girl."

Justin nodded in understanding.

She went on, "And who do you suppose did it? The
wife?"

"No, Mrs. Thaine was here in Wallport at the time of the
crime," Justin said.

"I don't believe in alibis," Mrs. Allwood said. "What
was she supposed to be doing here? Going to the cinema?"

"Well, yes, as it happens, she was."

"Doesn't mean a thing. Anyone can sneak out of a
cinema without being seen. You'll see, it'll be the wife they
arrest. What sort of man was this Thaine?"

Her questions ran on, on the lines that might have been
expected. Justin was thankful when, a cup of tea hastily
drunk, he and Doris were allowed to leave for Archersfield.

In the bus, however, Doris also plied him with questions.
Justin discovered that in describing himself as the friend
of a friend of Arnold Thaine's, he had created the impression
in the girl's mind that he was a friend of Mrs. Thaine's.
When he denied this, telling her that he had met Mrs.
Thaine for the first time the evening before, Doris immedi-
ately concluded that the friend was another woman in
Thaine's life.

She had no doubt at all, she told Justin, that there must
have been a great many women in the life of a man as
attractive as Arnold Thaine. The blush that went with her
saying this made Justin wonder a little about Kenneth
Hersey in London and to feel a little sorry for him. But he
also felt sorry for Doris, cooped up in an old-fashioned
hotel in Wallport, with no friends in the neighbourhood

and with nothing to do but to go about the country, sight-seeing all alone, and in the month of November too.

When they left the bus, he walked with her to the police station. On the way he told her that he would wait in the bar of his hotel, in case she should want to speak to him again after she had seen the police.

When he told her the name of the hotel, she said, "Yes, I know it. I had lunch there yesterday. But you weren't there then, were you ? "

" No, I was having lunch with a friend," he said.

" The—the friend you told me about ? "

" Yes."

" She must be someone you care for a great deal."

" Well, we've known each other a long time."

" Kenneth and I have known each other a long time," she said. " He was in the army in India during the war. D'you think it's a good idea to marry someone you've known a long time ? "

" I can't tell you, I've never been married," he answered.

" Those are the people who generally tell one most," she said. " Of course, Kenneth and I didn't meet for several years, so it was almost like meeting a new person when we saw one another again in London. That can happen, you know."

" Yes," he said, " I know."

" When I spoke to him on the telephone," she went on, " I asked him to come down here, but he said he couldn't get away."

" What does he do ? "

" He's a schoolmaster."

" Well, they're busy men. Don't look so depressed about it. He'd have come if he could."

She was frowning. " I think people can always do what they *really* want to do, don't you ? "

" Not without exception, no."

" I do, I really do. Still, perhaps when he's had time to think about it . . . You'll be in the bar, you say ? "

" For some time, anyway."

" I'll come then, when I'm through here."

She went up the steps to the doorway of the police station.

Justin walked back to his hotel. He went straight to the bar, which, since it had only just been opened, was still almost empty. When he ordered his drink there was only one other person there.

From this person's attitude, however, his elbows on the bar, his head sunk on his arms, it might have been supposed that he had been there for hours, instead of only the few minutes that were possible. Recognising the stocky figure, the wide shoulders and the large, grizzled head of Lewis Brillhart, Justin slid his own drink along the bar and sat down beside him.

Brillhart looked up. The glass in front of him had not even been touched, yet Justin could have sworn that he was drunk. His eyes were red-veined, the lids were swollen and his face had a bloated, purplish look. If he was not drunk, then he had been crying.

He seemed to have difficulty, for a moment, in recognising Justin, then he muttered his name, seemed satisfied with having achieved this much, turned away from him and stared down moodily into his whisky.

Justin asked him, " Something happened ? " He was apprehensive of he knew not what.

Brillhart nodded.

" Yes, my dog's lost again."

IX

JUSTIN WOULD never have believed that such a piece of information could affect him as it did. Instead of relief and even amusement at what he heard, his mind was invaded by some horror that existed in Brillhart's and he found himself ready to believe that the loss of the dog might signify disaster of almost any magnitude.

To hide what he felt, he said in a falsely cheerful tone, " Well, cheer up, he'll turn up again."

" But where ? "

" He'll probably just walk in some time."

" No."

" Oh, come," Justin said, beginning to recover himself. " D'you mean a big brute like that never goes off on his own at times ? Why, I remember when we were children, we had a bob-tailed sheepdog that sometimes went off on excursions by himself that sometimes lasted for as long as three or four days. Then he'd trot in and settle in as if he'd never been away. The first couple of times he did it, of course, we got worried and thought he was lost, but after that——"

" No ! " Brillhart brought a clenched fist down on the counter. " If I tell my dog to stay at home, he stays. Besides, he was in the yard again and if he's in the yard he can't get out unless someone lets him out. That's what happened. It was like yesterday. Somebody came to the door of the yard and fetched him. And let me tell you this, it was someone he knew quite well, because I was in the house all the time and I never heard him bark."

" But what possible reason could anyone have had for doing that ? " Justin asked.

" A very simple reason," Brillhart said. " So simple that I begin to think I'm going mad when I think about it. I can't help knowing just why they came and fetched my dog away."

" They ? " Justin said.

" They—he—she—what does it matter ? I don't know who it was, but I do know why it was done. And that's why I'm going to stay here all the evening, where lots of people can see me, and then whatever they try to prove . . . But perhaps it's too late already. D'you think it's happened already ? "

" If I knew what you were talking about . . ."

" The murder, the murder ! " Brillhart's voice rose. " Yesterday they came and fetched my dog and shut him up in the same house with a murdered man. That was because they knew what everyone knows, that my dog and I are always together. So if my dog was there, I must have been there—don't you understand ? Only what they didn't know yesterday was that I was in London and that I could prove it. And so the plan failed. But to-day—what's going to happen to-day ? "

Justin's response to the drama of it was what his response nearly always was to excessive excitement in another person. He felt embarrassed and irritable and full of impatient commonsense. But these were feelings which he considered it necessary to control, since it was seldom helpful to express them. Drinking some beer, he remarked idly, " I saw your dog loose in the square yesterday morning."

Brillhart did not seem to hear him.

" No one's going to believe me, of course," he said. " I could go out into the middle of the square and warn everyone at the top of my voice, but no one would listen. You're hysterical, they'd say, you're a damned nuisance, they'd say, we've had one murder already and that's enough for sensible people like us——"

"I saw your dog loose in the square yesterday morning," Justin repeated more loudly.

Brillhart frowned heavily, trying to take it in.

" When ? " he asked abruptly.

" Around eleven, I think, or a bit later," Justin said. " He seemed to be quite on his own."

" How did you know it was my dog ? "

" I didn't. But when I saw him again in the evening, I remembered him."

" You saw him all by himself in the square in the middle of the morning ? " Brillhart, still frowning, checked up carefully on what he had been told.

" Yes."

" Then someone had already been to my house and let him out."

" Yes, for certain."

" Well, then ? " Brillhart seemed to think it proved his point.

" But it's unlikely that it was the same person who took him to the Thaines' house in the afternoon, or the evening, isn't it ? "

At first Brillhart's features set in sullen rejection of the point, then he nodded his large head slowly.

"You're quite right," he said, "quite right. It was stupid of me not to grasp what you meant. I'm too worked up to think properly. But who was it who came to my house, then?"

"Suppose it was Thaine?" Justin said.

"What makes you suggest that?"

"Didn't someone suggest it last night?"

"Yes, I believe so. Hester, wasn't it? But she didn't seem to have any reason for it. She said she was only guessing."

"All the same, Thaine went out during the morning, when apparently it was usual for him to stay at home."

"How do they know he went out?"

"Grace and Eagan both say so, don't they?"

"Well, I suppose if they *both* say so . . ." But there was something odd in Brillhart's prominent eyes as he said it. He picked up his glass, lifted it half-way to his lips, then set it down again. "It's possible, of course, that Arnold came to see me. I don't think I'd mentioned that he was going to London and there may have been something he wanted to discuss with me. But generally, if there was anything of that sort, he'd ring me up and ask me out to his house. He was a little—well, autocratic. If he did come looking for me, it must have been because he'd got something rather unusual on his mind."

"And haven't you any idea what that might have been?"

Brillhart sat silent, thinking.

Behind Justin, the bar-room door swung open and Justin looked round to see if it could be Doris Allwood already. But it was two elderly women in Sunday hats that nodded with flowers and veiling, who came in, seated themselves chattily in a corner and ordered port.

"No," Brillhart said, "but something does occur to me. If it was Arnold who came—*if* it was—then he must have had a reason for wanting to talk very privately. He could certainly have done that better at my house than at his. People were always wandering in and out there. For instance, just that morning, Grace and Ben. But I don't get many visitors."

"Suppose he'd wanted to talk privately about that row he'd had with Eagan the evening before," Justin said.

A snorting sound, that might have been a laugh cut short, came from Brillhart.

"You've been finding things out, haven't you? Who told you about that?"

Evasively, Justin replied, "It seems to be fairly common knowledge."

"Is that so? I didn't realise it," Brillhart said. "I haven't been talking about it. Anyway, it wasn't important."

"Wasn't important to whom?"

"To Arnold. That's to say . . . No, I don't think even Arnold would have worried about it."

"Why d'you say 'even' Arnold?"

"Because he was a touchy devil. Suspicious. Ready to jump at the idea that the people who really cared about him were most against him. You know the type. I don't mean anything really abnormal, but—well, difficult sometimes, definitely difficult, though perhaps not really more so than most gifted people. They all have to pay for their gifts somehow and the way poor Arnold had to do it was in distrust. He distrusted everyone more or less, except when he felt that he was completely dominating them, and that meant, of course, that he had no real friends. A lot of people cared for him a good deal, I think, but I doubt if he ever got any happiness out of it."

"So you do think he was gifted?"

"Good God, yes! Don't you?"

"I'm not sure that I've ever seen any of his work."

"Then I must show you—but what made you ask that?"

"Some stories that I've been told have been going about."

Again Brillhart made the snorting sound that he had made before, but this time, because of the set of his mouth, there was no suggestion of a laugh in it.

"Yes, you *have* been finding things out, haven't you?" he repeated.

"I haven't much else to do," Justin said.

" And of course we all want to talk." Brillhart gave him a long, considering look. " If I didn't talk, I'd go mad, and yet I'm afraid to talk to the people I know. All of us who are involved in this thing have found out suddenly how little we know about each other. But these stories—don't worry about them. They're just the sort of scandal that attach themselves to the name of any brilliant man."

" Haven't you any idea who began them ? "

Brillhart shook his head, but it seemed to Justin that his eyes were wary.

Again the door of the room swung open and several people came in together. But Doris Allwood was not amongst them. Justin glanced up at the clock. More time had passed, he thought for a moment, than he had realised, then he remembered that pub clocks are always fast and, comparing this one with his watch, he found that the clock on the wall was ten minutes ahead. Another deceiver. But in this case, the deception was so traditional that no one was ever taken in, unless, like himself, in a moment of forgetfulness.

" Brillhart, what did Thaine do when he really needed to know the time ? " he asked suddenly.

" He rang up TIM."

" Seriously ? "

Brillhart grinned. " So he said. I doubt it rather. I think he just shouted at Hester and she looked at her watch. . . . By the way, about those stories . . ."

" Well ? "

Brillhart was looking rather dreamily before him. " It's a thing I've never asked her about, but it's always rather puzzled me. . . . Didn't it strike you as odd, when you were there last night, that there's none of Thaine's furniture in Hester's drawing-room ? "

It was the last thing that Justin had expected to hear from Brillhart.

" You're not suggesting that she's responsible for these stories ? " he said.

" *Hester ?* " Brillhart exclaimed in a startled voice. " Good lord, that isn't what I meant."

" What did you mean then ? "

It seemed to Justin that Brillhart took longer to reply than he needed.

Finally he said, "I oughtn't to have mentioned it at all. I know I'm talking too much. But I've got so many things churning around in my head and I can't talk to Grace or Ben. This afternoon, when I saw you in the square, I thought perhaps we could get together and I tried to stop you rushing off. . . . But I don't know, now I don't feel that it's right to talk, even to you. It simply feels disloyal."

"What did you mean about Mrs. Thaine's drawing-room?" Justin insisted. "At the moment you've talked either too much or too little."

"Why, I meant simply that she believes those stories," Brillhart said explosively. His face reddened as he said it. "She'd never admit it, but isn't it obvious, isn't the evidence there? Until about a year ago that room was furnished like the rest of the house, as a sort of permanent exhibition of Arnold's things. And then one day out it all went and all the Victoriana came in instead and Hester would never say a word about why she'd done it, except just that she felt more at home with it. But there was a sort of anger in her when she said it, I could tell that, even when I hadn't the faintest idea what it was all about. Then I began to run into the stories myself and I thought . . . Well, as I said, I feel sure the poor girl had heard them and that though she probably never said a word about it to Arnold himself, that was her way of showing what she thought."

"But if the stories weren't true, and Thaine hadn't even heard them," Justin said, "he can scarcely have understood the gesture."

"Exactly," Brillhart said, "and that's something that puzzles me a good deal, because he wasn't a person to accept a thing like that in his own home simply because Hester wanted it. In the ordinary way, I'd have expected him to raise hell and for all of us to hear about it."

"Meaning," Justin said, "that he *did* understand the gesture."

"I don't know, I don't know," Brillhart said hurriedly. "These are just things I don't understand and that I haven't been able to talk over with anyone. And I know I oughtn't to be talking about them now. But the thing that really puzzles me, the thing I can't sort out at all, is . . ."

"Well ? " Justin asked as Brillhart suddenly stopped.

Brillhart took a handkerchief out of his pocket and wiped his forehead. Excitement had been growing in him again until it was almost back at the pitch at which it had been when Justin found him in the bar.

"The thing I want to know," Brillhart said, " is—from whom would she believe a story like that about her husband ? Because she wouldn't just take it from anyone, would she ? She'd only listen to someone she trusted as a person and as—well, as someone who understood such things."

"Meaning Ben Eagan ? "

"I don't know, I don't know. I only wish I did. Ben seems so decent. And there was another man—there was a row and he left—but I hardly knew him, he left soon after I got here, and I've no reason to be suspicious of him. Don't think I'm trying to make you think it's him. But it has to be somebody——" He broke off as sharply as before, but this time he was staring past Justin at the door.

Justin looked round. Grace stood in the doorway.

She looked weary and heavily depressed. With her shoulders drooping, she came across to them and slumped on to a stool at the bar.

"I thought I'd find you here," she said to Justin. She ignored Brillhart completely. "Where've you been all the afternoon ? I kept ringing up here, but they said you were out."

"I went to Wallport," Justin said.

"Whatever for ? "

"I got restless." Though he wanted to tell Grace about his discovery of the girl in red, for some reason he did not want to do so in front of Brillhart.

She sighed heavily and leant her elbows on the bar. Justin asked her what she wanted to drink and it took her a moment to make up her mind that she wanted brandy. Brillhart suddenly got up and went out. As he went, Grace muttered, "Thank the lord for that."

Justin thought that Brillhart probably heard her, for he let the door swing shut behind him with a little more violence than was normal.

Justin said irritably, " Why d'you have to do that ? It doesn't help matters."

She shrugged indifferently. " What's he been telling you ? "

Though Justin was in two minds about Brillhart and about the things that Brillhart had been telling him, he found that Grace's attitude put him almost automatically on Brillhart's side. He decided to say nothing about the hints that Brillhart had dropped concerning Hester Thaine and Eagan.

" That his dog's lost again, for one thing," he said.

" I hope it turns up dead."

" He thinks it means that someone else is going to turn up dead."

A corner of Grace's mouth lifted contemptuously. " Why did you really go to Wallport, Justin ? "

" To look for a girl in red."

" Find her ? "

" Yes."

She raised her eyebrows. Then she opened her bag, fumbled in it for a comb and turning towards a mirror on the wall, began to fidget with her hair. She was very unconcerned.

" If her story's true," Justin said, " she came into the affair as accidentally as I did and things don't look too good for the woman in brown."

" What is her story ? " Grace went on combing her hair, though what she did to it seemed to make little difference to its appearance.

Justin told her the whole story that Doris Allwood had told him, besides the manner in which he had discovered her.

When he had finished, Grace only observed drily, "Talkative girl."

" Rather," he agreed.

She began tapping with her comb on the edge of the counter.

Leaning towards her and dropping his voice, he said, " Grace, don't you see what this can do to you ? "

" You believe her, then ? " she said.

" Why not ? "

" I think she told you too much."

" Wait till you see her," he said.

" Is she so very attractive ? "

" I thought so at first. Now I'm not so sure. But she'll be in here presently. She's the sort of person who never knows when to talk and when not to. Besides, if she's really been in India all her life, when did she get to know Thaine well enough to want to murder him ? Was he ever in India ? "

" I'm sure he wasn't. He hated travel. But d'you know what amazes me ? "

" What ? "

" The way everyone seems to be taking for gospel truth the evidence of a doddering, half-paralysed old man, who probably really spent half the afternoon asleep, but won't admit it."

" No, that isn't the amazing thing," Justin said. " The amazing thing is the way you won't face one or two simple facts."

" They aren't so simple, Justin. Either that girl's lying, or the old man is."

" Because, you mean, in spite of what you said before, Thaine was already dead when you got to the house."

She snatched a quick, terrified look round the room to see if anyone had been listening. But the conversation in the bar was fairly noisy and it seemed unlikely that Justin's low voice could have been overheard.

He went on, " So either the girl must have killed him, never having seen him before, or else at least one other person must have gone in and out of the house before you got there. But both of those possibilities still put you in the house with Thaine dead, Grace."

In a voice even lower than his, so that he only just caught the words, she said, " There's still another possibility."

"Yes, that you did the thing yourself. But you don't have to persuade me that you didn't."

She shook her head. "I didn't mean that."

Picking up her bag, she opened it to replace the comb with which she had been fiddling, then she stood up. But her hands were shaking and she failed to close the catch on her bag. Swinging open, it half-emptied itself on the bar in front of Justin.

A piece of paper lay there before him. It was covered with a fine, clear handwriting that he immediately recognised. A few words, perhaps because he was already familiar with them, sprang up at him, ". . . After our conversation, I think the only thing for me to do is to resign. . . ."

X

GRACE SNATCHED the paper up and crammed it back into her bag.

Justin did not try to stop her.

"Have another drink, Grace," he said.

She hesitated, then without arguing, climbed back on to her stool.

"So you saw it too," he said.

"Yes."

"Brandy again?"

"Yes, please."

He gave the order.

Opening her bag once more, she took out the letter.

"You may as well read it," she said. "I knew you'd seen it. It was because of the way you looked last night when you saw it that I went back for it. From where I was standing, I could only see that it was a letter to Arnold."

"I suppose Eagan knows you've got it."

"No, he doesn't."

"When did you go back, then?"

"This afternoon. He was over with Hester, so I just walked in to the cottage and took it."

" You mean it was still lying around on the table ? "

" Of course. I knew it would be, that's why I went. Can't you see he's the sort of person who never puts away anything ? And that could make trouble for him with the police, so I went and got it."

" He won't be very pleased."

" No." She smiled bitterly. " Aren't you going to read it ? "

He felt an immense reluctance to do so. " Has it anything to do with all this ? "

" Read it and see."

Justin unfolded the letter and read it quickly.

" Dear Arnold, after our conversation, I think the only thing for me to do is to resign. No doubt I should have done this some time ago, when I realised what was happening to me. To that extent you were right in what you said to me. But in all the rest you were wrong. I repeat that I never forgot that Hester was your wife and I swear that I never said anything to her that could not have been said if you had been there. If she is aware that I am in love with her, which I do not believe she is, then it can only be because . . ."

At that point, the letter stopped. At that point, presumably, Eagan had been interrupted in his writing by the arrival at the cottage of Grace and Justin, with the news of Arnold Thaine's murder.

Justin folded the letter again and returned it to Grace. She put it back into her bag and snapped it shut, firmly this time. They both sat silent for a while, elbows on the bar, while they thought their own thoughts.

At last Justin said, " So that was what the quarrel was about."

" Yes."

" How long have you known about it ? "

" That Ben had fallen in love with Hester ? Not really for sure until I read that letter. I thought . . . But never mind what I thought."

" You must have known for sure when he and Thaine quarrelled."

" No, Ben denied it then. He was quite convincing."

" But you'd some suspicion of it earlier ? " He was thinking of Grace's changed attitude to Hester Thaine, as Hester had described it.

" Well, perhaps. I didn't want to believe in it though."

" Does Hester know about Eagan's state of mind ? "

" Of course she does."

" Because Eagan did tell her ? "

" Probably."

There had been a sullen sort of pain in Grace's voice as she answered these questions. Her eyes met Justin's for a moment now, then she leant her head on her hand, hiding most of her face from him. But before she did this, he had seen the misery in it and several things that he had half-guessed the evening before in Eagan's cottage became clear to him.

He did not say anything, but Grace knew him too well to doubt that this had happened, and when she spoke again, he could tell from her voice that she had let some of her defences fall.

" I always do it, don't I ? " she said in a hushed, dreary voice. " You've seen it happen to me before with men like Ben, gifted, helpless sort of men, years younger than me. Even Dick was younger than me, though not much. But Ben's so many years younger than I am that I've felt there was something horrible in loving him, particularly when I thought for a while that he was falling in love with me. I've tried with all my strength not to let him know what I felt, but I think he does, all the same. I'm always so bitter and hard with him now, which I never used to be."

And Brillhart knew too, Justin thought. Here was Grace's secret of which he had spoken.

Justin dropped his hand on top of Grace's and held it.

She went on, " Someone once told me that I've always gone on looking for Dick, but that isn't it at all. For one thing, Dick was as tough as could be. He'd a slim, pale, rather girlish look, but he'd a will like iron. We used to have awful quarrels sometimes, and it was always I who gave in."

Justin remembered those quarrels. Dick DeLong had

described some of them in detail, almost hysterically bent on convincing himself that his will had in fact been stronger than Grace's. He had been one of those very helpless men, of the kind that had always attracted Grace so strongly, who flared up intermittently into rages of self-assertion, but who in the main give love in exchange for support and protection.

But Ben Eagan, Justin thought, was not like that. Ben Eagan really had that inner toughness that Grace mistakenly remembered, or pretended to herself that she remembered, in Dick DeLong. Ben Eagan would always be very wary of any woman in whom there was such a passion of protective domination as there was in Grace. Justin felt very sorry for her.

"How d'you think Thaine found out about it ? " he asked. "Did Hester tell him ? "

"Brillhart told him," she said.

"Isn't that just a guess ? "

"You'd call it guessing, but I'm certain of it."

"How did he find out, then ? "

"By using his eyes. They're very sharp ones."

"Grace, what is it you really have against Brillhart ? "

She did not answer, so after a moment Justin asked, "Where does he come from ? How did you get to know him ? Where's his wife and what's the matter with her ? "

To the last question, Grace replied, "She's insane. She's in a lunatic asylum."

Justin caught his breath.

"And after his fashion, he's loyal to her," she said grudgingly. "He goes to see her regularly. If—if it's true that he was in London all day yesterday, that's what he was doing. He goes about once a month. I don't know just what the trouble is, or how bad she is, or if there's any hope for her, because you can't rely on what he tells you. Sometimes he talks wildly about wonderful improvements in her condition and how he'll soon be bringing her here to live, and sometimes he talks quite coldly about the case being of course incurable and of his having got used to it and not really caring any more."

" All in all, the way most of us would behave in the same circumstances," Justin said. " How long ago did it happen to her ? "

" I think it must have started during the war, while he was overseas. He came back and found her in a pretty queer state, but he didn't realise then, so he says, how serious the case was and thought that he could pull her round by himself. So he didn't bother about trying to get a job, but stayed with her all the time and attempted his own line of psychotherapy. That sounds fine, I know, yet somehow, whenever he talks about that part of it, I get the feeling that really he's furiously angry with her because it didn't work. And whenever he talks about psychiatrists in general and blasts them to hell for being incompetent, I get the feeling that he's furious at the idea that any other man could know more about his wife, or about anyone, for that matter, than he does. Understanding people is Brillhart's speciality. But anyway, in the end he dumped her in an asylum and decided that since his savings had run out, he'd better look for a job. And that was when I met him."

" Was that down here ? "

" No, we picked each other up in a pub in London. I'd gone there to meet someone who didn't turn up and Brillhart spotted that I was getting upset, waiting, and started talking to me. And he had such a sensitive, warm, perceptive way to him that I took to him immensely. We met again the next evening and the evening after. Then when I came back here, he started ringing me up every night, and one day he simply turned up here. He told me all about himself, that he was a painter and sculptor and that before the war he'd begun to do quite well and had even had an exhibition of his own, but that since the trouble with his wife, he'd lost the heart for it and that the only thing he could bring himself to do was tinkering with bits of carpentry. I tried to get him to show me some of his pictures, thinking that perhaps he could be set going again—after all, I know lots of people and I might have been able to help him—but the only thing he'd ever show me were little tables and cabinets and so on that he'd made. And they were really very good indeed. So then I introduced him to Arnold."

"And the paintings, what were they like when you did see them?" Justin asked.

"They didn't exist, isn't that what I've been telling you all along? But he'd summed me up very carefully. He knew that I was interested in painting, he also knew that I knew Arnold. And he thought that I'd go farther to help him with Arnold if I thought he was a starving artist than if I thought he was just a plain, straightforward cabinet-maker. I was quite coldly and deliberately exploited. But besides all that, you know, being a cabinetmaker, a very sound one but still a mere craftsman, isn't good enough for Brillhart himself. He's got to believe that if he'd had a chance, he'd really have painted those pictures. And sometimes I think he almost believes he has painted them. But in fact, he hasn't a trace of talent or originality or even of taste."

"There's taste and originality of a kind in that little house of his," Justin said.

"Oh, that was all Arnold. He always handed out his advice on such things without waiting to be asked and Brillhart had the sense to take it."

"And how did you find all this out?"

"Slowly and bit by bit. Realising that the paintings simply didn't exist. Seeing a sketch he'd done of a chair he was working on, and realising that he hardly knew how to hold a pencil. Meeting one or two people he'd known, who dropped hints and warnings. And finding out about his war record too. Why is it that people of that kind always have to make out that they were in Intelligence, doing incredibly secret and dangerous things? In fact he was in the infantry right through the war. As if that isn't good enough for anybody—but not for Brillhart, you see. He had to be dropped alone by parachute behind the Jap lines, and contact secret agents in Warsaw—sometimes he forgets what he told one last and gets his geography a bit mixed up. It's always the kind of story that you can almost believe in a pub, after one drink too many, but looks a bit too garish in the light of day. All the same, I was never much worried by those stories, perhaps because I never did quite believe in them. But I did believe in the paintings. And the irony of it all was that it was quite unnecessary. If I'd seen some of his real work, and if I'd known the story of his wife and why and how badly he needed money, I'd have done everything I could for him with Arnold and ended up by keeping my liking and respect for him. But people like that can't ever assess that sort of thing. I think his whole mind's made up of distrust of other people and contempt for them."

"Distrust," Justin said. "I seem to have been hearing that word a good deal."

He was feeling very uncomfortable. He had the unwillingness of most reasonably tolerant and fair-minded people to believe evil of anyone whom he had known, face to face, and found even moderately agreeable. Going over Grace's story in his mind, he wondered if some interpretation different from hers, or at least with a different emphasis, might not be made of Brillhart's behaviour, so that it could seem less calculating and therefore more forgivable. Grace, after all, was a highly emotional witness, with a deep and possibly exaggerated grudge against Brillhart.

But to avoid having to come to a conclusion on the matter, Justin switched the conversation back to Ben Eagan.

"When you rushed over to the Thaines' yesterday morning," he said, "was that because you were expecting more trouble between him and Eagan?"

She nodded, swirling the last few drops of brandy about in her glass.

"I'd seen Ben start out, you see. I can see that cottage from the landing window upstairs. I didn't do anything about it at once, but then I started to worry, thinking about the row the night before, and after a bit I decided to go over to see if I couldn't smooth things out. But on the way I met Ben coming back already, saying that Arnold and Hester weren't up yet. I told him that was preposterous, because they're both pretty early risers, so then Ben told me that in that case, Arnold must be out. He asked me what the time was, saying his watch had stopped and that he hadn't the faintest idea what time of day it was."

"Yes, he told me all that," Justin said. "He said he'd been to the Thaines', but that finding no one about and the fire not yet lit in the studio, he'd concluded it was very early in the morning, until he'd met you and you'd told him what the time really was."

Grace frowned. "I don't know what he was talking about. The fire was lit all right. I went into the studio and stood in front of it, thinking perhaps Arnold would come back in a few minutes. But then I realised you'd be arriving at any moment, so I dashed back home."

"It sounds a bit as if Eagan never actually went to the Thaines' house at all," Justin said.

"That could be, I suppose. He might have changed his mind before he got there and turned back. But I don't know why he shouldn't have said so."

Justin suddenly became intent. "But you did go in, you say? You went in and waited in front of the fire?"

"Yes," she said.

"D'you remember the clock over the fireplace, the one that was stopped by the shot?"

"Yes, of course."

"Well, do you remember the time it showed when you were in there in the morning, waiting for Thaine?"

"No, I'm afraid not."

"Think hard," he said eagerly. "Just try to recall what you saw. It might come back to you."

"No," she said, "that won't be any use. For one thing, I hadn't got my glasses and I'm much too short-sighted without them to see a clock high up on the wall."

From just behind them, a voice joined in the conversation, "Good evening, Mrs. DeLong. Good evening, Mr. Emery."

It was Turkis.

Both Grace and Justin started. Though Justin was sure that Turkis had been standing there for only a moment and that during that time nothing had been said that was unsuitable for the ears of a policeman, he felt a prickling sensation up his spine.

" I was told Mr. Brillhart was here," Turkis said. " Have you seen him ? "

" He was here, but he left some time ago," Grace said.

Justin, recovering himself, added, " He was worried about his dog."

" I know," Turkis said. " I came to tell him we've found it."

" That'll be a load off his mind," Justin said.

" Will it, I wonder." Turkis's face was grim as he spoke. " We found it dead in a ditch up at Fallow Corner. The poor beast had been poisoned with strychnine."

XI

Turkis did not stay talking for long. To a question from Justin about Doris Allwood, he replied that he had just put her on the bus back to Wallport. Then he went out again in search of Brillhart.

Grace left soon afterwards.

Justin had one more drink, then went to the dining-room, where he ate a very bad dinner, but in such a state of abstraction that he scarcely noticed what he was putting into his mouth. His mind was busy with arithmetic. But his calculations, although they were simple enough, left him dissatisfied, for the sum added up plainly to Doris Allwood's being guilty of the murder of Arnold Thaine, and that, so far as Justin could tell, did not make sense.

During the long interval that occurred between the removal of the cold, tinned, sausage meat and the appearance of some pink blanc-mange, he scratched figures on the tablecloth with the prong of a fork.

The figures were 1.5, 7.50, 11.15, 4.30.

One-five was the time, according to the lantern-clock over the fireplace in the studio, when it had been stopped by the bullet.

Seven-fifty was the time that that same clock had shown when Ben Eagan looked into the studio during the morning.

Eleven-fifteen was Justin's rough guess at the real time of that visit of Eagan's, a guess he had arrived at by putting together the stories told by Eagan and Grace about what had happened during that morning. Eagan had said that he had been to the Thaines' house, had looked into the studio and come away again, meeting Grace on the way home. Grace had said that she had met Eagan, had gone on to the studio, waited there a few minutes, then recollecting that Justin's bus was due, hurried back to Fallow Corner. Since Justin's bus had left Archerfield at twenty minutes past eleven and the drive to Fallow Corner took about twenty minutes, it seemed to him reasonable to suppose that Grace had left the Thaines' house at about half-past eleven and Eagan perhaps a quarter of an hour earlier.

However, if the clock on the wall had shown the time as seven-fifty when it was in reality eleven-fifteen, then when it showed the time as one-five, it would in reality have been four-thirty.

Four-thirty was the time at which the old man in the cottage claimed to have seen the girl in the red coat go into the Thaines' house.

There was just one possible flaw in these calculations. Justin, absently scooping up spoonfuls of blanc-mange, was considering this flaw when, with a start, he realised that the woman who had just walked quickly up to his table was not the slow-footed waitress, but Hester Thaine.

As he got to his feet, she said breathlessly, "No, don't get up. I didn't mean to interrupt you. I'll go away and come back later. That, is, I'll go and wait for you in the lounge—that is, if you're free. I'd like to talk to you, if I can. . But it isn't really particularly important."

She fled out of the dining-room before he could stop her.

He followed her at once and found her standing in front of the fire in the empty lounge, wrenching off her fur-backed gloves. She had a green woollen scarf knotted over her head and was wearing an old, worn, mannish-looking khaki raincoat, tightly belted round her narrow waist. Her elegance, it seemed, was reserved for her home and what she wore out of doors unimportant to her.

As Justin joined her, she gave him a nervous smile, then knelt down suddenly on the hearth-rug, holding her thin hands out to the blaze.

" I'm frozen—I've been cold all day," she said. " It's got into my bones. I feel as if I'll never be warm again. That's shock, I suppose."

He asked her if she would like coffee and when she agreed, he added brandy to the order.

" But isn't there anything you want to do ? " she asked. " Are you sure I'm not stopping you getting on with it ? I'd like to talk to you, but it isn't really important. To-morrow would do as well."

" I've nothing whatever to do but sit and wait for something to happen," he answered. " I'm glad you happened."

" Yes, one just has to sit and wait. . . . But I don't see why you should have to." Still kneeling, she went on holding her hands out to the flames. " After all, you'd never even met Arnold. Have they told you that you must stay, or are you staying because of Grace ? "

" Because of Grace, I suppose."

" Do you think you can help her ? "

" Do you think that she needs help ? "

" I didn't mean that." She began to tug at the knot of the green scarf, wrenching it off her head. " I meant . . . I meant . . . I'm not sure what, exactly. I've somehow got into a state of panic I can't control and my thoughts are all tangled up. Grace does need help, of course. Anyone can see that. But that's nothing to do with Arnold's murder. I mean . . ." She gave it up. A convulsive shudder ran up her thin body.

" Are you still staying all alone at that house ? " Justin asked.

" Yes," she said.

" Are you sure that's wise ? "

" No, I can hardly bear it, but I don't know what else to do."

" Haven't you any friend you can go to—other than Grace, if you're afraid of going to her ? "

She thought for a moment, then shook her head.

" But I've nothing against Grace—don't think that," she said. " I mean, I'm not afraid of her, I don't suspect her, nothing like that. It's just that in a way it's easiest to be alone."

" In spite of the panic ? "

" Yes, I'll get over that. I'll have to."

" But why be so tough with yourself straight away ? Couldn't you give yourself a little time to recover ? "

" No. No, really this is best."

" But——"

" Please ! " There was a spark of anger in the word which she tried immediately to smother with a smile. " You're wondering what's brought me here, aren't you ? Well, there are two things. One is that I wanted to thank you for talking to Ben this morning. He came to see me in the afternoon and he told me all about that quarrel in the pub. As I thought, it wasn't really anything important. The second thing——"

Justin interrupted. " He told you the cause of the quarrel ? "

" Yes, and as I expected, it wasn't really a quarrel at all, though it may have sounded like one."

" What was it, then ? "

" Just an argument." She smiled again. Her gaze, meeting his, was quite candid. " I told you how worked up Arnold could get in an argument that wasn't of the least importance. In fact, that was what he liked about it, the getting worked up and the shouting and the pounding the table with his fist. I've seen it happen so often."

" But did Eagan tell you the subject of the argument ? "

" Oh yes. But it sounds so absurd now."

" May I know what it was ? "

" It was about whether or not Iago was a convincing character."

For a moment Justin felt completely bewildered. Her tone sounded perfectly natural and her eyes were neither evasive nor too steady. If she knew how little truth there was in what she had said, she was a liar of outstanding talent. But he failed to see at first what purpose the lie could serve.

Apparently his expression betrayed some of his feelings, for she gave a slight laugh.

"I said it sounded absurd. But it's just the sort of thing that Arnold could argue about as if he'd got a personal grudge against Iago."

"So he was the one who thought that Iago was convincing?"

"D'you know, I'm not quite sure. I'm not quite sure that Ben told me. Anyway, that isn't important, because even if it was Arnold, a day or two later he might easily have taken the opposite side and said that Iago was just a mechanism for creating Othello's jealousy of Desdemona and that anyone with so little motive for such evil actions couldn't really exist."

"So," Justin said thoughtfully, "they talked about jealousy, he and Eagan?"

"I suppose so. If you talk about Othello, that does tend to come up, doesn't it?"

"And no doubt they'd have discussed whether Othello himself was a noble or a base character and whether or not he could possibly be excused for his suspicions of Cassio."

"I suppose so."

The waitress came in then with the coffee and the brandy. Hester drew away from the fire, standing up and unbuttoning the shabby raincoat, revealing the same severe black dress that she had worn in the morning. Then sitting down and pouring out the coffee that the waitress had placed on a table near her, she went on, "The other thing that brought me was that I heard you'd discovered the girl in red, who came to our house in the afternoon."

Confusedly, Justin nodded, taking the cup that she held out to him.

He had understood by now the reason for her story. But he was still undecided as to whether she had told it in good faith, or whether she had lied knowingly, after having helped Eagan to concoct the lie. And up to a point, Justin thought, it was a good story. Those people in the pub who had eavesdropped on the quarrel, like the woman who had spoken to Hester in the Wallport market, would find it difficult to prove that the quarrel had been about Arnold Thaine's own jealousy and not Othello's. But there was an obvious flaw in the story, which was that it would hardly convince either Grace or Brillhart.

Could Hester and Eagan count on their loyalty, then? Could Hester be sure, or could at least Eagan be sure, that Grace and Brillhart would confirm the lie?

Hester was speaking again. "Is it true? Did you find her?"

"The girl in red?" Justin helped himself to sugar and stirred his coffee. "Yes."

"And?" she asked quickly.

He told her of his meeting with Doris Allwood. She listened with an intensity which Justin thought might come from her anxiety over what she might discover concerning the girl's relationship with her husband.

"And that's all?" she said when Justin finished.

"That's all."

She relaxed noticeably. "And do you believe it?"

"The police will check it all, of course," he said.

She nodded thoughtfully, her gaze becoming faraway, as she pursued some thought of her own.

"There's just one queer thing about it," she said, "and that is that there wasn't the faintest chance that Arnold would have sold her the clock with the cupids. Or any of them, if it comes to that."

"Couldn't he have been joking? The girl herself didn't seem sure that he was serious."

"I suppose it's just possible, but it doesn't sound like him. And you really think she'd never seen him before?"

"Well, she and her aunt had only been in Wallport a week. Before that, I think, they were in London, and before that, up to some time in the summer, Miss Allwood was in Bombay. Was your husband ever in India?"

"I don't believe Arnold ever want abroad in his life," Hester said. "And certainly he hadn't been to London for months. It really does sound as if she can't have known him."

"It does, I think."

"But that means . . ." She looked at him as if she wanted him to end the sentence for her, saying what this information could mean to Grace. But he did not help her out.

Picking up her glass of brandy, she took a small sip from it, her body twitching slightly as the spirit went down.

"Why didn't you and Grace ever get married?" she asked.

He laughed.

"It never seemed to arise," he answered.

"But weren't you ever in love with her?"

"Perhaps, at one time, in a way."

"And why did nothing happen?"

"As I remember it, she was in love with her own husband just then."

"Was she very attractive as a girl? I've always thought she must have been."

"Yes, in a rather individual sort of way. At least, I thought so."

"And did she know you were in love with her?"

"I think so. Anyway, as soon as she saw what was happening to me, she hastily supplied someone else for me to fall in love with."

"And did you?"

"Up to the hilt."

"I bet Grace regretted it." She smiled. "And when you came down here, was it your own idea, or had Grace asked you to come?"

"It was my own idea."

"You just wanted to see her again?"

"Well, I'd been abroad for a long time and when I got back I could find hardly anyone I'd known before, and suddenly I couldn't stand that any more, so I came looking for Grace."

She sipped a little more brandy. It had already brought a trace of colour to her cheeks.

"I wish I had a few really old friends," she said. "But somehow I let myself get out of touch with them all when I married. I used to have lots of friends and I

suppose they're somewhere around still. . . . Mr. Emery,
I don't believe Grace killed my husband."

The abruptness of it took him by surprise. Then he
realised that this was what she had been trying to find
some way of saying for the last few minutes.

" Have you told her that ? " he asked.

" No, I can hardly do that without letting her know that
I've been at least considering the possibility."

" But of course you have been. And also the possibilities
of Ben Eagan, Lewis Brillhart and the girl in red. Perhaps
even of me."

" Yes, I've wondered about you and where you really fit
in," she admitted. " And Ben. But now Miss Allwood's
proved that it couldn't have been Ben, since she saw Arnold
alive a long time after Ben did. And Lewis was in London,
visiting his wife. That policeman told me they've checked
on that already and there's no doubt of it. So that leaves
Grace, out of our little group here, and I suppose she could
have been the woman in brown. But I just don't believe it.
You see, if she was, she *has* to be the murderess, unless this
Allwood girl is lying."

" Perhaps," Justin said slowly, " Doris Allwood *is* lying.
Perhaps she's scared and is afraid to say that she found your
husband dead when she got here."

" No ! " It came out passionately and Hester's cheeks
flamed. " It wasn't Ben. I know it wasn't."

He looked at her sombrely. But he was pursuing his own
thought of a moment before, wondering why he had not
thought of it sooner. If Doris Allwood had spoken the truth
about having had no connection of any kind with Arnold
Thaine, yet out of some idea that she might save herself
from becoming involved in an unpleasant situation, had lied
about finding him alive, then Eagan and not Grace must be
under suspicion. It was this, Justin was now sure, that
Grace had instantly recognised when he had told her in
the bar what Doris Allwood had told him.

At the same time he remembered that some question
concerning Doris Allwood had been knocking at his mind
for some time. Now it came to him.

"Mrs. Thaine, what time did you light the fire in your husband's studio yesterday?" he asked.

Hester looked astonished.

"Why, at the usual time, I think," she said, "about eight in the morning."

"And would it have been alight still, say about half-past eleven?"

"Oh yes, I think so. I didn't leave the house until about half-past ten and I made the fire up just before I left."

"Was your husband in the studio then?"

"Yes. But what's important about the fire?"

"Just that Eagan says that when he went over to your house about a quarter-past eleven, it was out."

"No, it couldn't have been."

"Grace also says it was alight."

"Yes, it was. But I still don't see . . ."

"It's only that it's an odd sort of thing to get wrong, isn't it?"

"I suppose so." She spoke impatiently, seeming to find no sense in this line of questioning. "But d'you know what I think we have to do, Mr. Emery? I think we've got to look for someone who's outside our circle here. I think we've got to look for someone out of the past."

"Are you thinking of someone special?"

She hesitated for an instant, then said, "No." But as soon as she had said it, a restlessness got into her and she stood up, hastily buttoning up her coat.

"No," she repeated more loudly than she had yet spoken. "And if I were and yet hadn't a shred of evidence against the person, I couldn't say anything, could I? But I suppose it has to be a woman, doesn't it, a woman in brown?"

"That's how it looks at the moment," he agreed.

"Then d'you know what I think you should do if you want to help Grace?"

He shook his head.

"Go and talk to the old man in the cottage," she said. "Find out if you think he really saw what he thinks he did." She held out a hand to him. Though she had been

sitting so close to the fire, her fingers were still cold. " Good-
night, Mr. Emery. Thank you for listening. You've been
very patient with me."

She left quickly.

A curious sense of resentment overcame Justin after she
had gone. He thought that that last suggestion of hers had
probably been the real object of her visit and that she had
had other reasons besides the ones that she had given for
making the suggestion. He thought that she had decided
that he was someone she could use, without being too
explicit about the end for which she was using him, though
the end was simply the safety of Ben Eagan, which Justin
wished she had dared to admit. However, he remembered,
women who live with such men as Arnold Thaine tend to
become secretive and over-diplomatic. It was probable also
that her distrust of himself was only a reflection of her
distrust of Eagan, against which her undoubted but perhaps
still unadmitted love for him was not yet strong enough to
guard her. The little flare of resentment dulled. A slight
feeling of desolation took its place. It was almost as if
Justin envied for the moment the people whose lives had
been engulfed by the tragedy, whose strong feelings of love,
or suspicion, or hatred of one another tied them close in a
relationship of fear and danger, from which he, in his
safety, was excluded.

But besides himself there was another spectator on the
sidelines. Doris Allwood. It was perhaps part of Justin's
dissatisfaction with himself just then that she had allowed
herself to be put on the bus back to Wallport by Turkis,
instead of coming to find Justin in the bar. He wondered
if he would ever see her again and also, briefly, whether by
any chance he minded if he did not.

He wondered for a rather longer time about the truth of
her story and about Eagan's. For if Eagan's story about his
morning visit to the Thaines' house was accurate, then, as
likely as not, Doris Allwood was not a spectator but a
murderess. If the clock above the fireplace had really shown
the time of Eagan's visit as ten minutes to eight, then the
bullet must have been fired into it at half-past four, the time

at which, according to her own and the old man's testimony, Doris Allwood had been in the house.

But was there any reason for believing Eagan's story? At least part of it was untrue. The fire in the studio had not been out at the time. Both Hester and Grace had been sure of that and both women were far more concerned to protect Eagan than to cast doubt on anything he had said. To say the fire had been out, however, was such a senseless inaccuracy that Justin was inclined to believe that it could mean only one thing, which was that Eagan had never been to the Thaines' house at all that morning.

But in that case, why should he say that he had? Whom had he thought it necessary to deceive? Where had he really been that morning?

As soon as Justin asked himself these questions, a possible answer to them all occurred to him. Eagan must have been walking towards the Thaines' house about the time that Hester had left it. Had they met somewhere then and talked? Talked of the murder on which they had decided? Confirmed their arrangements?

Justin sprang out of the chair and took a few violent paces up and down the room.

It would have been the easiest thing in the world for Eagan to say that the time on the clock was whatever he chose, and he had in fact not mentioned the time until after he had heard of the existence of the girl in red, an unknown girl, an outsider, about whose fate he could perhaps be indifferent. He had then given the time on the clock in the morning as the one that would point suspicion directly at her.

Justin was beginning to think that he saw light.

But then his pacing stopped and he stood still in the middle of the room, staring uneasily before him.

Doris Allwood herself had said that Arnold Thaine was alive when she called on him. If that were true, then Grace remained the only suspect worth considering, for Eagan's lie about the clock could have been calculated to protect Grace rather than himself. In fact, that was as good an explanation of the whole series of events as any.

Unless someone had entered the house whom the old man had not seen . . .

So perhaps Hester Thaine was right and it was important for Justin's own peace of mind that he should pay a visit to the old man the next morning.

XII

NEXT MORNING, while he was still at breakfast, he was told that he was wanted on the telephone.

It was Doris Allwood calling.

" Were you annoyed with me for going straight home last night ? " she asked.

" Yes and no. Why did you ? " he asked in return.

" Well, I'd begun to feel rather queer," she said. " You know how it is. The shock of a thing like that doesn't really strike you at first. But when the police were through with me—that inspector was very nice, but he went over and over the same thing until I wanted to scream—I stood up and for a moment I thought I was actually going to faint. So I decided perhaps I'd better go straight home. I hope you didn't wait long."

" I waited till Turkis came into the bar and happened to mention that he'd put you on the bus," Justin said.

" Oh dear, I'm so sorry. Then you *are* annoyed. That's a pity, because I wanted to ask you . . ."

As she hesitated, Justin thought that if what she wanted to ask him was to go and talk to somebody on her behalf, for reasons which she did not choose to explain fully, he would simply put the telephone down and return to his cooling scrambled egg.

" I wanted to ask you if you could come over to Wall-port to-day to have lunch with Granny and me," the girl said.

Perhaps if the intimidating old woman had not been included in the invitation, Justin would have seen his way

H

to accepting it promptly, but as it was, he thought for a moment, then said, "There's someone I have to go and see this morning. I'm not sure how long it will take."

"That friend of Arnold Thaine's you told me about?" the girl asked.

"No, as a matter of fact, it isn't."

"Is it Mrs. Thaine?"

"No."

"Oh dear, I don't mean to pump you. It's no affair of mine. Well, would you come over to tea, then?"

"Thank you," he said.

"There's a bus about three. Can you come on that?"

"Yes. But suppose something should crop up so that I can't?"

"Just telephone. I'll be in all the afternoon. I'm so glad you're coming."

She rang off. Justin returned to his breakfast and the newspapers.

From these he learnt nothing about the murder except that the police were anxious to interview a woman in a brown raincoat, who had been seen to enter the Thaines' house at five-fifteen on the day of the crime.

After breakfast, Justin went by taxi to the cottage where the old man lived. He had noticed it the day before, when he visited Hester Thaine. It was a trim little thatched cottage, with leggy rows of brussels sprouts in its carefully kept garden and only a small meadow dividing it from the Thaines'. Probably the cottage had once been occupied by the gardener who took care of the garden of the big house. White lace curtains masked all the windows.

When he knocked at the door of the cottage, a hoarse voice from inside shouted something at him that he did not understand, so putting a hand on the latch, he pushed and the door opened.

The voice shouted again: "If you're another of those reporters, I've had enough of you!"

"I'm not," Justin said.

"Oh—oh, you ain't?" The voice sounded, if anything, disappointed. It dropped to a grumbling mutter. "Come in then, whoever you are. But I ain't buying nothing, nor selling nothing."

Justin stepped inside a little kitchen.

The voice went on, " You'd be surprised the things people come here trying to get me to sell. Sometimes it's the very roof over your head. Or the cover off your bed. Or the clock in the corner that's stood there since you was born. Yes, Mr. Whoever-you-are, that very clock over there. Many's the time Mr. Thaine himself tried to buy that clock off me. What d'you think of that ? "

Justin, feeling that the old man was still hoping against hope that he was a journalist of some sort, drew a chair up to the table. He let the old man go on talking. He knew that there was nothing to be gained by hurrying to explain who he was or the purpose of his visit.

" Smoke ? " he said presently, holding out a packet of cigarettes.

" Thankee." A yellow hand reached out. " Later, if you don't mind." The old man tucked the cigarette away in the breast-pocket of his dressing-gown.

It was a shabby, but had once been a fine camel-hair dressing-gown. It was rather too large for its wearer, which made Justin wonder if it might not originally have belonged to Thaine. Under it the old man wore a striped collarless shirt and a pair of blue and white flannel pyjama trousers. His wrists and hands were very thin and he held one shoulder higher than the other, with his head a little to one side, as if he were partially paralysed. But the eyes in the deeply-lined, yellowish face were clear and intelligent. He was garrulous but not incoherent. That it would be possible to dismiss his evidence because of senility, Justin did not think probable.

It took the old man about twenty minutes to reach the point of asking Justin directly why he had come.

" Well, I have a certain connection with some of the people involved in this case," Justin said, " and I've been wondering if you'd be so good as to let me take a look at the Thaines' house from the window of your room. I should be most grateful if——"

"Ah," the old man put in, "you're a lawyer, eh?"

Justin made a vague gesture and did not reply.

"They've all took a look through that window," the old man said. "All the police and the reporters and Mrs. DeLong——"

"She's been here?" Justin asked quickly.

"Not half an hour ago, and trying to make me say, like the rest of them, that I dropped off for a bit during the afternoon. But it won't do. I never go to sleep in the afternoon. If I do, I don't get no sleep at night, and I'd rather have my sleep at night, when there's no wireless to listen to, than maybe miss a good programme in the day-time and then lay wide awake in the dark with nothing to do but think. No, if you've come to ask me didn't I nod for a while, Mr. Whatever-your-name-is, you're wasting your time."

"Well, may I take a look at the room all the same?" Justin asked.

"Take a look where you please. It's through that door behind you. I don't go up and downstairs no more these days."

Justin thanked him and went to the door.

He found a small room, crowded with furniture. The large bed was near the window. To reach it, Justin had to edge round the wooden footboard, flattening himself between it and the bulky dressing-table. The window was small, square, tightly closed and covered with white lace. But when he looked out of it, he recognised that anyone lying in the bed would have a perfect view of the Thaines' house and garden, and not only of these but of the studio as well.

That destroyed a hope he had been nursing until then that even if the entrance to the house was visible from the cottage, the door, or at least the window of the studio might be obscured by the house itself, or by a shed or a bush. But, in fact, through his bedroom window the old man had been able to see the gate and the short drive up to the house, the front door and also the whole side of the studio that faced the house. If he had been as wakeful and watchful as he claimed he had been, no one could have entered the studio without being seen by him.

As presently Justin walked away from the cottage, he thought about the old man's remark that Grace had been to see him. Justin did not like what it seemed to mean and the feeling of exasperated anxiety that was roused in him whenever he thought over Grace's behaviour of the last two days, returned and sent him walking along in a nervous hurry, as if he thought that he could help matters by getting somewhere quickly. He was walking so fast and frowning so unseeingly at the ground just before him that he would have gone straight past the Thaines' gate without noticing Turkis standing there, if Turkis had not called out to him, " Going anywhere, Mr. Emery ? "

The gate was open and Turkis was standing with his hand on the latch. Whether he was just going in or coming out Justin could not tell.

" I'm not sure where I'm going," he answered, " but I've been to see the star witness."

" You look worried," Turkis said.

" Wouldn't you, if you were me ? "

" I'm worried enough on my own account." Turkis leant his elbows on the gate. " Just think it out, Mr. Emery. You may believe that old man is telling the truth, and so may I, but could I convince a jury of that ? A bedridden old man who's ready to state on oath that he never took his eyes off this house for a minute even."

" It would take more than a minute to get from this gate to the house," Justin said.

" But not from the house to the studio."

Justin considered it. " D'you mean there was someone in the house all the time ? "

" I haven't the faintest idea. But someone could have come up to the house from the other side, couldn't they, across the lawn at the back, and got into the house by the door or a window, then popped across to the house in much less than a minute ? "

" Wouldn't it have meant climbing a fence and walking across a flowerbed to get into the garden from over there ? "

" It would."

" Well, are there any tracks ? "

" Not a trace of one. But the rain could have washed them away."

" Are there any muddy tracks inside the house, then ? "

" Any number. But everyone who came into the house that day brought some mud in. Then again, the person I'm talking about might have been in the house all day, and possibly even the night before."

" Without Mrs. Thaine being aware of it ? "

" I didn't say that."

Justin approached the gate and leant on it too.

" Are you serious in making that suggestion ? " he asked.

" I'm serious in all of them," Turkis said. " They're the suggestions that can be made to discredit the evidence of that old man. I've got to be serious about them."

" But why are you telling all this to me ? "

" Perhaps I felt sorry for you, seeing you walking by with that look on your face. It may have seemed sheer humanity to set your mind at rest for the time being."

" D'you suppose you know what I'm actually worried about ? "

" Oh, I think so."

Justin feared that he did. " Well, I doubt if you've succeeded very far in setting my mind at rest," he said.

" Pity," Turkis said. " I meant well. However, I've some more suggestions you may care to consider. One is that the murderer almost certainly knew the whole lay-out here pretty well, but that the rain here let him down."

" I don't understand that."

" Well, imagine a stranger in the neighbourhood, walking up to the house in broad daylight, murdering Thaine and coming away again. Wouldn't that person be scared stiff that someone from the cottage would see him ? Wouldn't the mere discovery that there was a cottage so close make him delay his visit till after dark ? But anyone who knew the situation here would know that there'd be no one in the cottage but the old man and that he could be counted on to be in the kitchen, looking out in the opposite direction.

The only thing is, it rained, and the old man didn't think it'd be much fun watching the road, so he changed his mind and stayed in bed."

Justin nodded. "Yes, I see the point. But if the murder was unpremeditated?"

"Oh, I agree. In that case it isn't important. Only the murderer took a gun with him. A gun that we haven't found. So there's something else to help your peace of mind."

"You're very kind. But returning to the murderer's probable familiarity with the layout here, that's support for the innocence of Miss Allwood, isn't it?"

"Now it never occurred to me you'd be worrying about that," Turkis said. "I thought. . . . However, you're quite right. To know the habits of the people in the cottage would require a rather intimate knowledge of the neighbourhood, and I don't see, as things stand at the moment, how she could have acquired it."

"But I suppose a murderer is sometimes plain stupid and doesn't take precautions."

"Frequently. But all the same, there's a tendency for murder to be a deed of darkness. There's something rather deliberate and thought out, it seems to me, about murder by daylight."

"Darkness—or dusk," Justin said thoughtfully.

"Exactly," Turkis said. "So in spite of everything I've been saying, I'd still very much like to talk with the woman in brown, who got here just as the light was beginning to fail."

"She may know nothing at all."

"If you believed that, you wouldn't have that worried look on your face."

"You're building too much on my looks," Justin said. "I've spent a good deal of my life looking worried. About the dog, now?"

"The old man didn't see him, if that's what you mean. That low bit of hedge there would have hidden a dog."

"No, about the dog's death."

"You know as much about that as I do. Someone had fed it strychnine. And I'm afraid it's just as likely to have been the father of some kid who'd been scared by the dog, or someone whose pet peke had had its ears chewed off by him several times, as it is to have been the murderer of Thaine. I like dogs pretty well on the whole, but there's no denying the fact that that one was a savage, badly-trained animal, whom a lot of people would have been glad to have out of the way."

" And have you discovered who let him out of Brillhart's backyard ? "

" The first or the second time ? "

" Both times."

" The first time," Turkis said, " Thaine let him out. I don't know yet who did it the second time."

" So Thaine did go to Brillhart's house that morning ? "

" Oh yes, that's certain. He was seen by several people to go in by the yard gate. And he came out again without bothering to close the gate behind him and the dog ran out after him. But I can't tell you why Thaine went there. According to Brillhart himself, it was very unusual."

" So I understood. Well, thanks, Inspector, for your information and your attempt at consolation."

Justin moved away from the gate.

Turkis did not move. " Mr. Emery," he said.

Justin paused again.

" If I were you, Mr. Emery, d'you know what I'd do now ? " Turkis said.

" Yes," Justin said, " you'd go back to Australia."

" Australia ? Well, I'm not sure about that. They tell me the pubs shut at six. No, I was just thinking you might be going to see your friend, Mrs. DeLong, and I was thinking of what I'd say to her if I were you."

" Meaning that it's something a detective-inspector can't say for himself ? "

A slightly injured look appeared on Turkis's face. " If that's how you're going to take it . . ."

" No, go on," Justin said. " At the moment I'm ready to listen to good advice."

" Well, I'd tell her that murder creates an unwholesome atmosphere. I'd tell her that most people start behaving

queerly, once they've breathed it for a while. And I'd tell
her that a person who's killed once hasn't necessarily got
the disease over for good. He can get it a second time."

"In other words, this is a warning?"

"Don't you think she needs one, considering how she's
acting at the moment."

Justin tried to keep his face and his voice non-committal.
"Do you actually think she's in danger of some sort?"

"Don't you?"

"It hadn't occurred to me."

"Come now, Mr. Emery."

"It's true. That's to say . . ."

"Ah, you'd thought of the danger she might be in from
the police." Turkis said it rather too casually for his tone
to sound quite right to Justin. "But there are other dangers
to consider, aren't there, to a woman who doesn't tell what
she knows? In the circumstances, I'd say a friend had a
certain duty."

"You are so very kind and thoughtful," Justin said.
"Thank you again."

He turned sharply and started walking away down the
road. He was angry, yet he really did not know with whom
or why, for the thought went with him that kind and
thoughtful was just what Turkis, in his way, probably was.
However, he had succeeded in creating in Justin a state of
nervous tension far worse than that which he had been in
when he left the old man in the cottage. And that, Justin
thought, had been entirely intentional.

He had an impulse at first to thwart Turkis by not going
near Grace that morning. But by degrees, as he walked
along, he managed to shed the mood that his talk with Turkis
had engendered and reaching the next crossroads, he took
the turning to Fallow Corner.

For some reason, when he did so, it did not occur to him
that he might not find Grace alone, but when he reached her
house, he saw two cars besides her own standing outside her
gate. The sight nearly made him walk straight on, for the
things he had been preparing to say to her were not things
to be said in front of an audience. But then curiosity made

him turn in at the gate. He walked up to the door and rang
the bell and when no one answered it, remembering that
the door was generally left unlocked, he turned the handle
and went in.

As soon as he was inside the house, he knew why his ring
had not been heard. The air was loud with angry voices.
They came from the sitting-room, the door of which was
not quite closed. One voice, a man's, but shrill with rage,
rose high above the others.

" I will not, I will not answer such accusations. I have
never, on any occasion, said such things. What gain would
there be for me ? What motive could I have ? Of all people,
I'm the one who stands to lose the most by Arnold's murder.
I had a job, I've lost it. Lost it and everything—yes,
everything ! "

The voice was Brillhart's.

Another voice replied, " No one's accusing you of Arnold's
murder." The voice was also a man's, but one that Justin
had not heard before. The anger in it was expressed in a
quiet but grating sarcasm. " If you were in London at the
time, as I understand can be proved, you couldn't very well
have murdered him. But I do accuse you of something
which in my view is almost as bad."

At that point, Justin pushed open the door of the sitting-
room and went in.

XIII

GRACE WAS in the room, standing at a window, looking out.
At the sudden silence, she turned her head with a jerk. She
did not look at all pleased to see Justin.

Brillhart was standing in front of the fire. His arms were
stiff at his sides, his hands clenched. There was rage in
his bulging eyes.

There were two other people in the room, a man and a
woman, sitting side by side on a sofa. They were of about
the same age, perhaps thirty-four or five, and without

being in the least alike in feature or colouring, they created a curious impression of resembling one another. It came from the way they both sat, rather stiffly and on the defensive, from the way they both raised their eyebrows as they looked at Justin, from something superciliously angry and yet scared in their expressions. The resemblance was of the kind that is sometimes acquired by married people who see a great deal of one another, but otherwise lead fairly solitary lives.

The woman was the taller of the two. She had a round, pale face with tidy, inexpressive features and smooth, thick, brown hair, parted in the middle and wound in plaits round her head. She was wide in the shoulder and full-bosomed. She wore a scarlet blouse, a skirt of ruby red that clashed boldly with the blouse, no stockings but a pair of green woollen ankle socks and low-heeled, lizard-skin shoes. She sat with her large, muscular hands, ornamented with a broad, Victorian wedding-ring, clasped round her crossed knees.

The man was slighter than the woman, with more angular, more restless features. His hair hung over his forehead in untidy curls, his skin had a muddy look and there were patches of bristle on his long, sharp chin. He wore a pale brown corduroy jacket, a green flannel shirt and shapeless flannel trousers. He was taking rapid puffs at a cigarette, the end of which he had mangled with his lips to soggy pulp.

Grace made curt introductions. The man was Julian Morse, who was Ben Eagan's predecessor as assistant and pupil of Arnold Thaine. He now had workshops of his own in a village on the far side of Wallport. He and his wife Rhona had come to see Grace because they believed they had information which might be relevant to the murder of Thaine.

When Grace said this, Brillhart cried out, " Information ! If you call that relevant information, you might as well accuse Arnold's clocks of telling the right time ! The only ' relevant ' thing these people have said so far is that they themselves were here in Archersfield on Saturday."

" To meet Arnold," Julian Morse said in his harsh, sarcastic voice, " by appointment."

"And it's certainly taken you a long time to come forward with this 'information' of yours," Brillhart went on passionately. "The news of the murder was in the Sunday papers and in the news on the wireless, yet you've waited till to-day to come here with your 'information.'" He exaggerated the word with flaring scorn each time he said it.

"We have no wireless," Rhona Morse said quietly, "and we do not take a Sunday paper. We'd heard nothing of the murder until Hester rang us up late last night."

"*Hester* rang you up?" Brillhart said incredulously.

Rhona Morse nodded. "And afterwards Julian and I discussed what we ought to do. We had no particular love for Arnold, as you may imagine, and we would just as soon have stayed out of it, but we decided that it was our duty to tell the police what we know. Only first, we thought, we would tell what we know to Grace, to see if she had any advice to give us concerning it. We've often taken Grace's advice in the past and generally found it helpful." She had a composed, colourless way of talking, but her eyes did not match it. They were restless and anxious.

Grace explained to Justin, "Rhona and Julian say that they had an appointment with Arnold at Brillhart's house on Saturday morning. But their car broke down on the way and when they finally arrived, there was no one there. So they started for the Thaines' house and on the way they overtook Arnold who was walking home through the rain. He got into their car and they had their talk there. Then they dropped him at his gate and drove off home."

Justin had sat down.

"Was there any reason why you couldn't have arranged to talk to him in his own house?" he asked the Morses.

"We both of us prefer not to go into his house," Rhona Morse said, "after the things he said to Julian on the last occasion that he was there, nearly two years ago."

"However," Morse added, "it was Arnold's own suggestion that we should meet at Brillhart's house."

"Knowing that he would be away in London that day?" Justin asked.

"Oh no, he didn't know that," Morse replied. "If he

had, we should have made the appointment for another day. The object in meeting there was that Arnold thought Brillhart should be present at our conversation. Grace had the same feeling, which was why——"

"Which was why she felt she was safe in asking me here to be insulted and humiliated, with no way of defending myself!" Brillhart roared.

"Which was why," Morse went on, "she asked him to come out here as soon as she heard what Rhona and I had to say, the reason for this being that we are making a certain accusation against Brillhart and she felt he had the right to hear it."

"It's just like her, just like her!" Brillhart cried. "And once I thought you were such a good, such a truly *good* woman, Grace. Oh God, how am I ever going to trust anyone again?"

"Then we're quits, aren't we?" Grace said distantly, turning to look out of the window again. "My trusting nature has suffered some damage at your hands, Lewis."

"But why, why? Why do you believe these things about me? Emery——" He swung round on Justin. "Have I ever slandered Arnold to you? Didn't I tell you last night, when you asked me about it, that Arnold was a fine artist? Didn't I tell you that the stories going round about him were completely false?"

"You did," Justin agreed. He was feeling sorry for Brillhart, who looked old to-day, almost an old man, an excitable, angry, desperate, old man.

"One way of spreading a slander," Morse said, "is to be continually denying it."

"Oh, is it?" Brillhart said, breathing hard. "And what's the best way to suppress it, then, when a vicious, jealous mind has set it going? Repeat it, perhaps, agree with it, embroider it?"

"Do I understand," Justin said, addressing Morse, "that you claim you have evidence that Brillhart was responsible for these improbable stories about Thaine?"

"Yes—and you must understand, Mr. Emery, that I have a rather personal interest in the matter," Morse said. "It was because of these stories reaching Arnold Thaine and his believing that I was responsible for them—and after all, since the substance of them was that I was a genius and Arnold a fake who was unscrupulously exploiting my talents, it was a natural enough thing for him to believe—it was, as I said, because of this, that he turned me out, calling me all the vilest things he could think of and ordering me out of his workshops then and there. It's also why he's done everything he could to injure me in my work ever since."

"But this evidence," Brillhart said, "that you claim you have, what does it amount to but the gossip of several people, which you've picked up here and there and which you choose to believe, because it happens to suit you and not because you can prove it? There'll be as much gossip around that you've disregarded because it was inconvenient to you."

"The evidence," Morse said, "is that the same stories have been circulating about Arnold and Ben Eagan and though no one can remember who first told them the stories, my wife and I have discovered several people who are ready to swear that Brillhart was going about very busily denying them, even to people who'd never heard them. I agree that this is far from conclusive, but Rhona and I considered it of sufficient interest to lay before Arnold, so that Ben Eagan at least should not suffer the same treatment at his hands as I did."

"Very kind of you," Brillhart said. "Very moving. And will you suggest any reason why I should spread such stories about Arnold, who'd given me back a will to live that I'd almost lost—no, I won't say that, or anything else like it, because you'll only sneer at the expression of such feelings —but I will ask you what I had to gain by turning against him? Why should I risk fouling my own nest? Who else is going to give me work on a par with what Arnold gave me? I'm not a young man, like you or Ben, with the chance ahead of me to make a name for myself. I lost the chance of that that I might have had by going to fight in a war. And now I'm simply a middle-aged man who's never achieved anything. But Arnold didn't mind that. He had a use for me. He gave me work I could do and take a pride in and he paid me enough so that I could spare my poor wife the indignity of staying in a common lunatic asylum. Why—will you tell me why, in God's name—I should risk destroying all that for the pointless satisfaction of spreading some incredible slanderous stories about him ? "

He did not wait for an answer, but stormed out of the room.

Still looking out of the window, Grace said sombrely, " Yes, why ? I'd like to know the answer too. What makes a man do a thing like that ? "

" Are you sure he did it ? " Justin asked. In fact he was more or less convinced by now that it was Brillhart who had spread the slanders about Thaine, but Grace's violent concentration on the point made him want unreasonably to come to Brillhart's defence.

Rhona Morse stood up, shaking out the full folds of her red skirt.

" But his motive was obvious," she said. " The stories were against Arnold, but calculated, when he heard them, to make him believe that they'd been spread by Julian— and these recent ones, of course, by Ben Eagan. And as for fouling his own nest, people like Brillhart never expect to be caught out. They never expect to have to answer for the damage they cause. And, after all, in the first instance, he didn't have to. He succeeded in getting rid of Julian, expecting, I imagine, to step into his shoes. The arrival of Ben Eagan must have been quite a blow to him. Now I think we'll be going, Grace. We'll go to the police, then unless they tell us to remain, we'll drive home. It was nice to see you. Why don't you come over to us sometime ? " There was no change in her voice as she shifted from accusations to commonplaces and walked with a rather handsome, heavy dignity towards the door.

Grace saw her and her husband out to the gate.

When she returned, Justin asked, " Are those two particular friends of yours ? "

Grace gave a shrug of her shoulders. " Not really, but I believe them, all the same."

" Even if they're right, however," Justin said, " this information doesn't seem to have much to do with the

murder. It's true it supplies Brillhart with a motive of
sorts. I suppose if he'd spread those stories and Thaine
had found him out, he might have killed him in a sort of
terror of the possible consequences. In fact, it might even
have been in self-defence. Thaine was a big man, wasn't
he, and a fairly violent one? But still, Brillhart was away
in London at the time and it'll be best for us to accept
that."

Grace nodded, but gave a shiver as she did so.

"Why did you come here this morning, Justin?" she
asked. "Any special reason?"

"More or less special," he said. "But about that couple,
what sort of people are they?"

"Rather arrogant and a bit phony but fairly harmless."

"What's their relationship with Hester?"

"I don't know. Why?"

"Well, is it possible that she could suspect Mrs. Morse
of the murder?"

Grace looked astonished, but thought it over before she
answered. "D'you mean because she telephoned them last
night?"

"Yes, and because she did that after saying to me that
she didn't believe you were the woman in brown, but
dropping a hint that she had an idea who the woman in
brown might be."

"So you saw Hester last night?"

"Yes. She came to see me after dinner, I think on
purpose to drop that hint and to get me to go and talk to
the old man in the cottage, to see if there wasn't some
loophole in his evidence."

"She's making quite a lot of use of you, isn't she?"
There was mockery in Grace's voice. "She sent you to
talk to Ben in the morning, didn't she?"

"Any objections?"

"Oh no. No, indeed. I'm making use of you too,
aren't I?"

"Grace, don't be a fool."

She laughed savagely. "But I've always told you, haven't
I, that I don't understand Hester, or what her motives are?

I always thought she was very much in love with Arnold. But now I begin to think that her extreme subservience to him meant that she felt guilty for not being in love with him. And I don't know anything about her attitude to Julian and Rhona. I didn't think she'd had any contact with them since they left, but I may have been wrong about that too. Of course, they've both published their loathing of Arnold pretty widely, with occasional threats to get even with him, but that's been going on for two years. I don't know of anything special that could have made them go further than that all of a sudden."

" Did Hester know the reason why Arnold kicked Morse out ? "

" I don't know. Why ? "

" Only that when I saw her yesterday morning she seemed to think that Thaine hadn't known anything of these stories."

" Well, it's possible that he didn't tell her much himself, so she thought he didn't know."

Justin thought back for a moment over his two interviews with Hester.

" I don't think it ever occurred to her that the stories came from Brillhart," he said.

" No," Grace agreed. " She's never seen through him, I'm fairly sure of that. He's always been very gentle and attentive to her, in a humble, worshipping way, and she wasn't used to it and naturally liked it."

" Are you quite sure she doesn't understand him better than you do ? "

Grace looked at him squarely and shook her head. " No, Justin, she doesn't. And to tell the truth, I'm worried about that. You see, I don't believe all his talk about being out of a job and having lost everything by Arnold's death and so on. I believe Arnold's death is going to be very much to Brillhart's advantage, temporarily, at any rate, because I think Hester will keep the workshops going, with Brillhart in charge. In fact, I don't see what else she can do. She hasn't any money of her own, that I know of."

" Unless she sells the clocks," Justin said. " Don't they represent a considerable investment ? "

"Perhaps they do. All the same, I think she'll try to keep the workshops going, using Arnold's designs. And then—well, later Ben will move in."

"You expect that?"

She shrugged with overdone indifference. "Now let's go back to the woman in brown," she said brusquely. "You're quite sure she's me, aren't you?"

"Well, isn't she?"

She turned away, looking into the fire.

"Yes," she said at last.

Justin felt that if he kept silence now, she would go on talking. He waited. But the silence lengthened out and he began to think that after all he would have to prompt her with more questions. At last, however, in a quiet, toneless voice, she continued. "You've been quite right all along, of course. I don't know why I didn't admit it straight away. I ought to have known I could trust you. I did go there about half-past five that afternoon and I found Arnold dead. And the dog was in the house, barking. And I jumped to the conclusion Brillhart had done it. Then when I knew it couldn't have been him, I thought it must have been Ben. And I went on thinking that until last night."

"What changed your mind then?"

"What you told me about Doris Allwood. If Arnold was alive when the girl called on him, Ben didn't kill him. Yet it isn't as simple as that, is it, because Arnold was dead when I called? So you're left with three possibilities, that a fourth person went into the studio whom the old man didn't see, that Doris Allwood, who'd apparently never in her life met Arnold before, suddenly went out of her mind and shot him, and that Doris Allwood actually found him dead, ran away as fast as she could, then got scared she'd get into trouble for doing that and decided to lie about the whole thing."

"In which case, Ben is still the murderer."

She did not answer.

"*Is* that what you think?" Justin asked gently.

"I'd like to believe in one of the other possibilities," she said, "but . . . Oh hell, Justin, he had the motive, he had the opportunity and he's been telling lies ever since it happened."

"So have you."

"Yes, but . . . well, you see now why I've been telling lies. I thought that if I could leave the identity of that third visitor uncertain, they couldn't fix on Ben right away. I suppose I was clumsy about it—but I'm always clumsy. And I suppose, if Ben did kill Arnold, that it was very wrong of me. But I'm not going to stop doing it—not yet."

"Grace—suppose you're in danger through doing it."

She lifted her head quickly. "Danger? Of arrest?"

"No-o," Justin said slowly. "Perhaps from Ben himself, or—or someone who thinks you know too much."

She shook her head contemptuously. "I don't know enough to be a danger to anyone. Where did you get the idea?"

"From Turkis."

She gave one of her sardonic laughs. "No doubt with instructions to hand it on to me. He's not as deep as you think he is if he thinks that that's the way to get me to talk."

"I'm glad that at least you've decided to talk to me," Justin said. "Perhaps we can begin to see where we stand now. For instance, about those lies of Eagan's. Tell me about them."

"Well, there's that stupid lie about the fire being out when he went over in the morning. Of course that means that he never went there at all. I don't know why he's been pretending that he did. I haven't any idea where that fits in, but I do know that it's a lie. Then there's his story that his interview with Arnold in the afternoon was so friendly and peaceful. If it was, why was he writing that letter to Arnold in the evening when we went to see him . . .?" Her voice trailed off and her eyes grew puzzled. "No, I'm getting mixed up. If he'd killed Arnold, or if he knew Arnold was dead, why was he writing that letter at all?"

"Suppose he didn't kill Arnold or know he was dead."

"Then he must still be lying about that interview being so friendly, because if it had been there'd have been no need to write that letter."

"What about the watch?" Justin asked. "If the interview wasn't friendly, would Thaine really have agreed to mend the watch for him?"

Grace gave him a quick look, looked away, then said suddenly, "Anyway, let's have a drink now and think about something else for a change. We'll never get anywhere by going on and on like this."

"Grace!"

She put a hand on the door of the cupboard, where she kept the drinks. "Well?"

"What do you know about the watch?"

"The watch?"

"You do know something you've not told me yet."

For a moment she remained standing quite still, holding on to the knob of the cupboard door. Then she jerked it open and began clattering bottles and glasses together.

"Yes," she said, in a voice that sounded as if she were furious with Justin. "I do. But if you tell this to any other living soul, I'll . . ."

"Never mind about that. What do you know?"

"That Ben didn't leave his watch there for Arnold to mend. You see, when I went in, the watch was on the floor beside Arnold. With the broken strap and all, it wasn't difficult to guess what had happened."

"You mean Thaine had torn it off Ben's wrist in some sort of struggle?"

"Of course."

"And it was you who put it on the table?"

"Yes."

"And that was why you insisted on going to see Eagan that night, to let him know that you'd done that?"

"Yes."

She held out his drink to him.

XIV

AFTER THAT, they talked of other things and presently Grace
produced some lunch on a tray. Then Justin told her that
he had an appointment in Wallport. Grace made no comment, but a few minutes later said, "You might have dinner
here when you get back. I think I'm going to see if I can
get hold of Ben this afternoon. If I can make him answer
a few questions, I'd like to talk over with you what he says."

Justin agreed to return and went out to catch the bus to
Wallport.

He had lost any desire he had felt earlier to see the two
Allwoods again. If he had not promised to go, he would have
disappeared for the afternoon into the local cinema. It was
showing a film about big game in Africa, and a poster of a
lion plunging straight into the camera, with what looked
like fire bursting out of its jaws, suggested a secure retreat
from human conflict. Indeed, the idea of going to see the
film seemed to Justin so tempting that he nearly persuaded
himself that it would be easy to forget Doris Allwood's
invitation. But he let the bus carry him past the cinema
and out into the country between Archersfield and Wallport.

Rain began to fall while he was in the bus, but it was not
like the heavy, monotonous downpour of Saturday. A gusty
wind drove the raindrops in little volleys against the windows
and made the stripped tree-tops toss wildly for a moment,
then left them quiet again. Because of the darkening sky,
lights began to show early in windows and car lights to
shine down the road ahead.

Justin's thoughts began to drift away from the problem
of Arnold Thaine's murder to another problem which
happened to have engrossed him a good deal during the last
few weeks, but which he found relatively pleasant to think
about. It was the problem of what kind of car to buy, now
that he was settled in England again. A tendency to day-

dream about bigger and better cars than he could afford
had slowed down the process of making up his mind, but
the bus journeys of the last two days had persuaded him
that the need for a decision was urgent. It was with thoughts
of this kind in his mind that he noticed a great and ancient
Rolls Royce pass by.

He noticed it with the mixture of amusement and rever-
ence that is roused in people by the sight of aged but still
nobly functioning machinery. He noticed how beautifully
it had been maintained, he noticed the stiff chauffeur in
uniform, he noticed too the entirely appropriate occupant
of the car, an old lady bundled up in furs, with a ponderous,
plumey toque on her head. But it was only when the car
had passed by on its way to Archersfield, that it dawned
on him that the old lady had been Mrs. Allwood.

This realisation disturbed him and made him impatient
to see Doris Allwood to ask her what had taken her grandmother to Archersfield that afternoon. Arriving at the bus
terminus, he found Doris there to meet him. She was
wearing her red coat with the hood up over her hair. She
seemed excited and worried and at once burst out into
hurried speech, " It's so good of you to come, Mr. Emery.
But d'you know, I've been trying to telephone your hotel
to tell you not to. It's all such a silly muddle. . . . But
anyway, the hotel people didn't know where you were, so
I supposed you'd started. I'm awfully glad for myself, of
course, and so long as you don't mind that it's just me
here . . . Because, you see, Granny suddenly decided
that she'd got to go and look into things for herself and I
couldn't stop her. I'm not sure what started it, but I've an
idea she had a telephone call. Perhaps it was from Inspector Turkis and he asked her to come, but I don't actually
know. She didn't tell me anything, she just ordered out the
car and went. And it was she who insisted on my asking
you to come over. I don't mean I wouldn't have done that
myself, but it's so stupid. . . . You aren't very annoyed,
are you ? "

She was clinging to his arm and hurrying him along
through the thin, driving rain.

"I'm relieved," Justin said. "Your grandmother intimidated me."

"Oh, I know what you mean," she said. "She does that with people at first. When I first arrived in England and went to live with her, I thought I'd never be able to endure it. I thought it'd be just like living with Queen Victoria when she wasn't amused. But it wasn't really. Granny's generally let me do just as I liked and when I got to know her a little, I found she was very good fun. But the trouble is partly that she's deaf and won't admit it, and sometimes when she looks at one stonily and imperiously, as if one had been making dirty remarks, it's only because she hasn't the faintest idea what one's said. What would you like to do now? Shall we have tea?"

Justin said that tea would be a good idea and Doris steered him to a large café in the main street of Wallport.

It was one of those places that at all hours of the day are packed to capacity with women laden with parcels from a riot of shopping. It was crowded now and very hot and the service was so slow that nearly twenty minutes passed before a waitress even approached their table to ask them what they wanted. But Doris seemed pleased with it. She wriggled out of her coat, dropping it over the back of her chair, combed out her fair hair, accepted a cigarette and said, "Will you mind it much if I talk an awful lot? I don't think I'm going to be able to stop it. It's such a peculiar feeling, getting involved in this affair and in a horrid sort of way I'm awfully excited by it. I hardly slept last night, I was so excited. Do you think that's quite disgusting, or do you think most people would feel the same sort of thing? I don't mean you, of course, you're so wonderfully calm. I know you take a balanced view of it. But I'm all churned up inside and I hardly know if it's because I'm frightened, which is silly enough in the first place, or horrified, which I suppose is what I ought to be, or just frightfully thrilled. And I've no one I can talk to about it, which makes it worse."

"My balanced view of things," Justin said, "comes from my being so churned up inside with just those feelings you've mentioned that they seem to cancel each other out and leave me numb."

"Oh no," she said firmly, "I don't believe that. You aren't like me. D'you know, I've even got a crazy sort of wish to dash over to Archersfield and try to get mixed up in it all ? "

"Which is just what I have done," Justin said.

"No, you've a friend who's in trouble. That's quite different. But in me it would just be thrill-chasing and nosy-parkering. Of course, I've been just a bit bored down here. I've nothing much to look forward to from day to day except Kenneth's letters and to tell the truth, they're a bit disappointing. He writes often enough, but he simply can't put things on paper, not things about his feelings, anyway. His subject is mathematics and so long as he can stick to figures and symbols, he's all right. But words, real words that tell you anything, seem to be beyond him." She rattled on.

In the warmth of the room some colour came into her cheeks and a glow into her dark eyes. She looked extremely young and the beauty that had struck Justin so vividly two very long days ago, when she had descended from the bus in the square in Archersfield and stood looking around her in the momentary sunshine, enveloped her again. In spite of her chatter, in spite of the noisy, crowded room, Justin began to enjoy being with her.

Tea and cakes appeared eventually. Doris attacked the cakes with gusto and when she had eaten three, thought that perhaps she would have an ice-cream. By that time she and Justin had quite stopped talking of the murder. Justin, in fact, had almost stopped talking altogether and even his listening was with only part of his mind. He found a strange peacefulness in the situation. It reminded him that there had once been a time when he had had no contact with murder and that the last two days were not eternal. It even seemed to promise him that such a time would come again. The tide of suspicion would recede and leave him free once more, free to leave Archersfield and to escape from Grace and her troubling claims on him. Just then he wanted most intensely to escape from her.

But escape to what?

A moment later he heard himself asking Doris how long she and her aunt were to remain in Wallport.

"For most of the winter, I think," she said.

"But will you be able to stand it? Won't you at least go up to London sometimes?" he asked.

"Well, I may, I suppose," she said. "But the trouble is, I don't really know anybody there but Kenneth, and he's working all day."

"I'll be there, anyway," he said. "Will you come up to London sometimes?"

He was not sure why he asked it so insistently. He was fairly sure that if she agreed to it, he would start hoping at once that she would forget all about it. But she did not agree to it, or even answer his question directly.

"I think I'd like to live in London," she said, "in one of those old houses up on Hampstead Heath. What d'you suppose makes people live in a place like Archersfield when they haven't got to?"

"Some people like to live in the country," he said.

"Yes, of course. And perhaps if you're married, with a home of your own and children and dogs and so on, it's not so bad. . . . But would you live in the country, if you had the choice?"

"I don't think so. I'm a rolling stone. I don't suppose I'll ever stay anywhere very long."

"You know, I think that's what I'm like too. But now tell me, all those people you know in Archersfield. . . . Don't they live a rather cut-off sort of life, never seeing anyone outside a small group of people?"

"Yes, I think that's so."

"So that they'd have to like one another an awful lot, or else they'd naturally get to hate one another."

"Perhaps."

"And if one of them had an awful lot of power over the lives of all the others, wouldn't they naturally get to the point where they all hated the thought of him?"

"What are you trying to say?" Justin asked. "That they all joined together to murder him?"

" Is it impossible ? "

Her tone was suddenly more serious and Justin, watching her, was surprised to see a look of far more positive intelligence in her bright dark eyes than he had expected to see there.

" Any reasons ? " he asked.

" If I say no, it's just my intuitions, you'll laugh at me," she said.

" Well, I sometimes suffer from intuitions myself," he answered.

" But one's own are always different from other people's. Well, my idea is—but it's just an idea, you understand— it's that there's something peculiar about both Mrs. Thaine and that man Brillhart having such good alibis for the time of the murder, and about that other man being clear of suspicion because I saw Arnold Thaine later than he did, when those are just the people who were in Arnold Thaine's power."

" You've been finding out a lot about them all," he said. " Where did you get all the details ? "

" From you and the papers and the inspector—mostly the inspector."

" How did the inspector take your account of your visit to Thaine ? "

" Well, he told me he'd have to check up——" She stopped. She sat up more stiffly. " Why did you ask me that ? Don't you believe what I told you ? "

Justin drank some tea. " I'm not absolutely certain that I do."

" Well ! " she said.

" I'm not saying I don't either," he went on. " But I've been wondering——"

She burst in, " So that's what you think about me ! And I thought you seemed such a—such a *sensible* sort of man. Is all this because I let you talk to me on the promenade yesterday afternoon ? D'you think that entitles you to say anything you like to me ? " She had turned rather white and her eyes were a blaze of anger.

" I haven't said anything yet," he said. " I was only going to say——"

" I know, that unless I can absolutely prove my story, it'll be quite easy to shift all the suspicion from your precious Mrs. DeLong to me. And I suppose that's why you agreed to come over and see me, and why you're sitting here having tea with me now. You're just waiting to trap me into saying something that'll help your wretched Mrs. DeLong. You don't care in the least what happens to me."

He frowned helplessly, and in a tone of exaggerated patience, said, " I'm certainly not trying to trap you or to shift any suspicion on to you. I'm quite ready to believe that you'd never seen Thaine before in your life and that you're not the sort of person who takes a gun along with you when you go to visit a complete stranger, but——"

" But you're going to suggest the gun was there on the table or something, and that I shot him because he molested me, or something like that ? Well, I didn't—he didn't— it all happened just as I told you. He was as nice as could be and told me to come again next day and I went away. But of course there was no one else there and I can't possibly prove any of it, and if you don't mean to believe me, I can't make you and I shan't even try ! "

Getting up swiftly, she caught up her red coat, tucked it under her arm and made rapidly for the door.

Justin started to follow her. Then he remembered that he had the bill to pay and by the time that he had accomplished this and threaded his way between the closely ranged tables and through the revolving door to the street, Doris Allwood had vanished.

He was not particularly put out, apart from the fact that he thought he had probably looked rather foolish in there in the tearoom, being abandoned so abruptly by the girl who was having tea with him. He walked along in the direction of the bus station, going slowly because of the crowds on the pavement, which were at their most dense, because offices and shops were closing. The rain was still falling and the wind that drove it slanting down the street made the evening very chill.

He had not gone far when he felt an arm through his and Doris Allwood, clinging to him, said, " I'm very sorry. I was silly in there."

Her hood had fallen back and the rain was falling on her bright, fair hair.

" It was natural enough," he said.

" No, it was just stupid," she said. " I know you weren't trying to frighten me. But the trouble is, you see, I do feel frightened. And that's stupid too, I know."

" I don't think you've anything to be frightened of," he said.

" No, I know, but all the same . . ." She was dragging as she clung to his arm. " The fact is, I can't get rid of a feeling that something horrible is going to happen to me, and I don't really believe in that sort of thing, I mean intuitions of danger and so on. Yet I can't get rid of the feeling and I don't think I've ever experienced anything quite so horrid. I know it probably comes from that morbid sort of excitement I was telling you about, but all the same . . ."

Justin stood still. " Doris, are you trying to tell me that you're afraid you may have accidentally picked up some knowledge which could be dangerous to you ? "

" Oh no," she said decisively. " No, I tell you, it's nothing real. I'm not even really afraid that my story won't be believed. It's just a feeling."

" And your story really is true ? "

" Of course it is. Are you going to start on that again ? What is it you're suspicious of ? What don't you believe ? "

" I was wondering . . ." But as he said it, he felt that there was no point whatever in continuing. Only as a salve to his conscience, so that he could assure himself that he had really done his best for Grace, he said, " I was wondering whether perhaps the whole story of your meeting with Arnold Thaine wasn't something that was spun out of this fear that you've been talking about—in other words, whether really you didn't find him dead when you went into the studio ? "

" Dead ? I find him dead ? " From the blankness of her gaze, it seemed that she hardly took in the meaning of it.

"And made up the story you told because you were too afraid of what might happen to you if you admitted the truth."

She took a moment to think, staring questioningly into his face. Then she said, " You aren't serious ? "

" Not very," he said.

" I understand. I see you had to ask the question."

" And the answer's still the same ? "

" It has to be. But is that so hard to believe ? "

He shrugged. " You see, if it weren't the same answer, it would even explain your present fear, because the murderer, of course, would know that you had lied and might suspect you of having noticed something that could incriminate him."

" But it wasn't like that at all. And I told you, my fear isn't reasonable at all, as that would be. It's just a—just a sense of disaster and horror. And perhaps it won't even be my disaster. It may just be something in the air. If you can't understand that sort of thing, forget I ever tried to talk about it. But really there'd be as much sense in my suspecting you of being mixed up in it all, as you believing all that about me."

" All right." He was thankful to be able to leave the subject. " Now I'd better go for a bus."

" I'll see you off," she said.

His last glimpse of her as the bus drove off a few minutes later was standing in the bus shelter, waving to him. She was smiling, yet she had a shadowy, apprehensive look about the eyes and he felt an unexpected pang of conscience at leaving her, as if her fears, real or imaginary, were somehow a responsibility of his. But he had already assumed as much responsibility for others as he felt inclined to take. Settling back in his seat, he opened the evening paper that he had just bought and began to read.

It was a local paper and though a good deal of space in it was devoted to the murder, it was reassuringly full of births and marriages, of notices of Conservative Party

meetings, auctions of furniture and amateur performances
of Gilbert and Sullivan. Presently Justin let the paper drop
and dozed a little.

When the lights of Archersfield appeared, he roused
himself, but he remained on the bus until it reached Fallow
Corner. As he got off it there, he saw the lights of a car
by Grace's gate. Justin's eyebrows went up sharply. The
car was a very large and ancient Rolls Royce, with a uniformed chauffeur sitting placidly at the wheel. The sight
surprised Justin very much indeed.

Hurrying up the path, he rang the bell. Then he rang
again. When there was no answer to the second ring, he
pushed at the door, expecting it to open, but this time it
was locked. Yet there were lights in the house, shining
behind curtained windows. After giving two more rings, he
turned and went down the path to the gate.

He spoke to the chauffeur. " Is Mrs. Allwood in there ? "

" Yes, sir," the man answered.

" Has she been there long ? "

" A goodish while. Two hours, maybe."

" And she told you to wait ? "

" That's right, sir. She didn't know how long she'd be.
Why, is anything wrong ? "

" I'm not sure," Justin said. " I've been ringing and no
one answers."

" That's queer."

" Yes. I suppose Mrs. DeLong's with her ? "

" Someone's with her. Someone let her in and I haven't
seen anyone leave."

" Well, I'll try again."

Justin turned back to the house. A moment later he
heard the footsteps of the chauffeur on the path behind him.
As Justin rang once more, the man said, " If you can't get
any answer at all, maybe we ought to snoop round the house
a little, just in case. With an old lady like her, you never
know what can happen. Her heart isn't too sound, and she's
all of eighty."

" Yes." The house was still as silent as before. " D'you
happen to have a light of any sort ? "

" I've got a torch in the car."

The man went to fetch it. When he returned, he and Justin went round the house together, looking for some other entrance.

They found one without difficulty. The back door of the house was not only unlocked but was ajar, banging a little when gusts of wind caught it. The kitchen inside was in darkness. The chauffeur's torch, sweeping around it, picked out a switch on the wall, and Justin, crossing to it, turned on the light and called out, " Grace ! "

After a moment, he called out, " Mrs. Allwood ! "

When no answer came to either call, the two men looked at one another, then together went swiftly through the house.

They found Mrs. Allwood immediately. She was in the sitting-room, seated in a deep arm-chair, facing directly towards the door. Her eyes stared fixedly at the two men as they stood, shocked into rigidity, in the doorway. The staring eyes bulged dreadfully. Her face was a hideous colour.

When they rushed to her, they found that her body was already cooling. A piece of wire was deeply embedded in the flesh of her neck.

Justin bent over her for an instant only, then started running from room to room in the house, shouting, " Grace ! Grace ! "

There was still no answer.

XV

HE DID NOT find her. All the rooms were empty, tidy and undisturbed.

Hurrying back to the sitting-room, he found the chauffeur at the telephone.

" I've just rung the police," the man said. He was white and shaken, but in control of his nerves.

Justin nodded, forcing himself to look at the terrible sight in the chair and to go closer to it.

He felt cold all over and that he was probably about to be sick, but his mind retained a detached and rather appalling calm. He noticed a small clock, with its glass broken, lying at the feet of the old woman, and his mind fastened on to this with a kind of chill annoyance, almost of irritability, as if this detail were just one thing too much to be borne.

Without touching the clock, he bent down to it so that he could see what time the clock showed. As he did so, he heard its quiet ticking and realised that it was still going. But the time at which the hands pointed was three minutes past one. Justin swore softly and violently.

The chauffeur bent down beside him to see what he was looking at, then straightened up, looking puzzled.

" Clock's wrong," he said.

" And why ? " Justin asked furiously. " There's no sense in it. Last time I was in this room, which was this morning, that clock was there on the mantelpiece and it was perfectly right. Why should it be wrong now ? "

" Perhaps the fall upset it."

" Why should it fall ? "

" Maybe it was used to stun her, then dropped there."

" There are plenty of heavier, handier things in the room."

" Then perhaps she snatched it up to defend herself, poor old lady."

" No," Justin said, " look at the way she's sitting. Some-one met her at the door, greeted her politely, brought her in here, helped her into that chair and when she was comfort-ably settled and possibly saying yes please, she would like a cup of tea, got behind her and strangled her."

" But then the clock——"

" Put there deliberately, I think—and put wrong deliberately."

" But why ? "

" I don't know, I don't know. As some sort of comment, perhaps. You've heard about the Thaine murder ? "

The man nodded.

" Well, that happened in a room full of clocks, all of them wrong."

" So you reckon the murderer might be meaning that clock to say like, 'Look out, don't meddle, or you'll get the same as this ' ? "

" Could be."

The man stared at Justin reflectively.

" Are you police ? " he asked.

" No, I'm a friend of the owner of this house. I was coming here to have dinner with her. My name's Emery."

" Mine's Morris." The chauffeur had withdrawn to the window and was staring out of it in a great impatience for the police to arrive. " And I was sitting out there, quietly reading my book, all the time she was being done in. Makes me feel queer when I think of it. She was all right, the old girl was. A bit high-handed, but she was all right. You knew where you were with her."

" Been with her long ? "

" Fifteen year."

" I'm sorry—you must feel it a great deal."

" That's right. But mostly I'm angry, me sitting there and her being done in, within call almost. Her a helpless old woman who couldn't lift a finger to help herself, and me sitting there, reading. . . ."

" You couldn't help that."

" No, that's right. But I got to go on thinking about it, all the same." He was a short, stiff, elderly man, with grey hair and sharp, clean-cut lines in a thin, serious face.

" Have you any idea why she came to this house ? " Justin asked.

" None at all. She just told me the address and we came here."

" Straight away, without any stop ? "

" When we got to Archersfield, we had to ask the way, but that's all."

" I meant, you didn't visit anyone else first ? "

" No."

Justin frowned in hopeless bewilderment. What, in God's name, had made Grace ask Mrs. Allwood to come here ?

What had Grace hoped to get out of her ? For the telephone call that Doris had mentioned, that had called Mrs. Allwood away so suddenly, must, presumably, have come from Grace. Furthermore, she must have made the call almost immediately after Justin had left the house to go to Wallport. She must have made it, knowing that he was on his way to Wallport, to see Doris and her grandmother.

And where was Grace now ?

He spoke to Morris again. " The person who let Mrs. Allwood into the house, can you describe her ? "

The man withdrew his gaze from the window. " Here they come," he said.

" The police ? "

" That's right. But I didn't see anyone, sir. Not that I was watching particularly. I'd just seen the old lady start hobbling up the path to the door, and I was reaching for my book, in among the maps and things, and I saw the door open, out of the corner of my eye like, and that was all. I didn't see whoever done it at all."

" The person who opened the door may not have been the person who did the murder," Justin said, his voice turning harsh without his intending it.

" No ? " Morris said sceptically and went towards the door as Turkis and a group of men walked in.

Turkis asked Justin and Morris a few rapid questions, then sent them out of the room to wait for more questions, when he should be ready to ask them. The two men settled in the kitchen. They smoked in silence, while heavy footsteps tramped through the house and voices spoke with what struck Justin unreasonably as a loudness and indifference quite improper in the presence of death. Morris seemed to feel the same, for once, when a door slammed, he started up with a look on his face that was not far from murderous. But he subsided again into his chair and mopped his face.

" I can't take it," he muttered. " The poor old girl."

Presently he stiffened up and exclaimed, " Miss Allwood!"

" Well ? " Justin said.

" I ought to call her, didn't I ? Or I ought to go there and break the news personally. She's all alone, she's got no one there she knows, and it was only last summer she lost her dad."

"I'd leave it to the police," Justin said.

All of a sudden he remembered his last few minutes with the girl in Wallport. He remembered the sense of vague fear that she had tried to express to him and the last glimpse that he had had of her, standing in the bus shelter, looking apprehensively forlorn. He wondered what this new tragedy, so much closer to her than the death of Arnold Thaine, would do to her. Death was coming close to her too often, forcing her to taste shock or grief too often, making her the butt of calamity.

But at least it was something that this last calamity could be clearly shown to have had nothing to do with her. Justin felt suddenly thankful that he had gone to that tea in the crowded café with the girl, rather than breaking his promise to her and going to the cinema.

It seemed hours before Turkis appeared in the kitchen. When he did, he asked the two men all the same questions that he had asked them before, their reasons for being there, the times of their arrivals, what had aroused their misgivings, how they had got into the house and just what they had done after getting inside. When they told him of the back door having been open, he went to it, opened it again and walked out into the garden. He remained out there in the darkness for some minutes, while the cold air of the November evening streamed into the kitchen.

Coming back, closing the door again, he said, "Well, that's how she got away."

"She?" Justin said.

"Mrs. DeLong," Turkis said, looking Justin in the eye.

"Now listen——"

"You listen!" Turkis cut in. "This is her house, isn't it? And Mrs. Allwood got a telephone call and came straight here to see her, and someone let Mrs. Allwood in and murdered her and vanished, while Mrs. Allwood's chauffeur sat in the car at the gate—vanished out through the door and the garden to the lane at the back. There was no difficulty about that."

" But make some sense of it, will you ! " Justin shouted. " Why did Mrs. DeLong want to see Mrs. Allwood ? Why should she suddenly go and murder her ? What in the whole world could she have had to fear from Mrs. Allwood, or to gain by her death ? " But his heart was heavy as lead while he spoke. Perhaps because of this, his bluster, in his own ears, sounded unconvincing. " How do you know it was Mrs. DeLong here in the house this afternoon at all ? " he asked. " It could easily have been somebody else."

" Yes, it could," Turkis agreed. He was looking at Justin rather as he had that morning at the gate of the Thaines' garden, in a way that suggested that for some reason he found Justin an object of pity. It was a look which roused in Justin, in spite of his effort to disregard it, feelings of rage and anxiety that rendered him more excitable than usual and more off his guard. " Yes, logically it could have been anyone. Almost anyone. But probably—what about the probability of it ? " Turkis stopped and turned his head sharply as a curious sound mingled with his words in the kitchen.

All of them heard it, a soft, choked, whimpering sound. As they listened, it came again.

Turkis took a couple of strides towards a door, which, as Justin remembered from his earlier visits, led into a larder. Turkis flung the door open.

Staggering, with her head held in her hands, Grace came out.

At the sudden light in her eyes, she gave a cry and shut them tight, but then opened them again and blinking rapidly, looked round at the three men in the kitchen. When she saw Justin, she took a quick step towards him, but immediately looked as if she were going to fall. Turkis caught her and slid a chair under her.

" See if the doctor's still there," he said to Morris.

" I'm all r-right," Grace stuttered. " I'll be all right in a minute. Where is he ? "

" Who ? " Turkis asked. Morris had hurried out.

" The one who was in here."

" Who was it ? "

"I don't know. I don't remember. I don't think I saw him. But I—I——"

Justin moved closer to her. "Don't try to talk till you've seen the doctor, Grace."

Turkis gave him a sardonic glance, saying to Grace, "You don't *think* you saw him?"

"No, I——"

"Grace!" Justin interrupted.

"I'm all right," Grace repeated, with the stubbornness of a person who is feeling really ill and is frightened by the feeling. "I'd like a drink of water, please. I expect I'll remember everything in a minute. Just now I can't seem to —I don't know—I came in here, but . . ." She gave a sharp shiver.

"All right, Mrs. DeLong," Turkis said, as Justin filled a glass at the tap. "Wait till you're feeling a little better. Here's Dr. Gerrard." He stepped back.

Grace drank the water hungrily, but then said abruptly, "Dr. Gerrard? What's he doing here?" Another thought struck her and she added, "What are *you* doing here? What's happened? That other man who was in here, who's he? Why is the house full of people?" Her voice had been rising more and more shrilly as she flung the questions at Turkis.

He did not reply, but gestured to the doctor, who had just come in, to attend to her.

The doctor's pronouncement, after he had given her a fairly lengthy examination, was that there was a bruise on the back of her head and another on her forehead, either of which might have been caused by a blow or a fall. He insisted on rest, because of the possibility of delayed trouble. Grace, looking by then more normal, pooh-poohed his advice, saying that what she wanted now was a strong drink of brandy and to be told what was going on in her house.

In surprisingly few words, Turkis told her.

She was already so pale that she had no more colour to lose, but blankness came back into her eyes so that Justin, who had been making infuriated attempts to stop Turkis and persuade Grace to go upstairs to bed, thought that she was about to lose consciousness a second time.

But, giving her head its familiar little shake, that set her short hair swinging, she seemed to dispel the cloud that was closing in on her mind.

" But why—why did she come here—why *here* ? " she asked.

" You telephoned and asked her to come, didn't you ? " Turkis said.

" I did? " she said incredulously. She said it not as if she were disputing the statement, but as if in surprise at hearing of some forgotten action of hers. Then she thought it over for a moment and said positively, " I did not ! Why ever should I ? I'd never even seen the woman."

" Didn't you telephone her, soon after Mr. Emery left here after lunch, and ask her to come and see you immediately ? "

" Certainly not." The sense that she was being in some way threatened seemed to help Grace's mind back to clarity. " I don't know a single thing about it."

" What about the person in here then," Turkis said, " the one who hit you—he did hit you, didn't he ? Can you tell me anything about that now ? "

" Not much. I don't seem to remember anything after I came in here," she said. " I don't remember being hit."

" That's quite normal," Justin said before Turkis could comment. " The mind often blacks out what happened just before the shock, as well as the shock itself."

" Thanks, Mr. Emery," Turkis said dryly. " I know a few elementary facts myself. All the same, it's natural I should ask Mrs. DeLong if by any chance she could tell me anything about her attacker."

" Sorry," Justin said, equally dryly.

Turkis turned back to Grace. " And you're sure you don't know who was in here ? "

" Oh yes, I do," she said. " It was Brillhart."

Justin sighed. He feared Grace's monomania was not going to be of much assistance to her at the moment.

"You said yourself you knew nothing about it," he said. "You didn't see him, did you?"

"No," she said, "but all the same . . ." Her voice faded into an uneasy mutter.

Turkis watched her intently for a moment, then asked, "Do you stick to that, Mrs. DeLong, that it was Mr. Brillhart who attacked you?"

"No," she said sullenly. "I expect he's got an impregnable alibi. I don't know who it was."

"Tell me what happened, as much as you can remember of it."

Grace propped her head on her hands, gazing woodenly at the table in front of her.

"Well, I'm not sure how long it was after Mr. Emery left to go to Wallport, I thought I'd go out——"

"Where?" Turkis interrupted.

"Nowhere in particular, just for a walk, to clear my mind and think things out a bit," she said.

In his own mind Justin added, to see Ben Eagan and confront him with a letter that he had written to a dead man.

"I was just going to go upstairs," she said, "to get my coat, when I thought I heard a noise out here. I do remember that quite clearly—a noise, but not worrying about it much, thinking perhaps a dog had got in and that I ought to come and see what it was. So I came and . . . I came into the kitchen and stood here a moment looking round and . . . and . . ." She stopped and moved one hand in a gesture of helplessness.

"All right," Turkis said. "And you still say you hadn't telephoned Mrs. Allwood? You weren't expecting her?"

"Of course."

"You know that if you had called her from here, that call could be traced. Calls from here to Wallport aren't automatic. There's a record of them."

Grace shrugged. "If the call came from this house, then it must have been made by Brillhart—or whoever it was—after he got here and knocked me out."

Turkis shook his head. "That would have been too late.

Mrs. Allwood's car passed Mr. Emery's bus when he was on his way in to Wallport. She must have started out, in fact, about the same time as he left here. So unless you were knocked out immediately after he left, it could hardly have been your attacker who made the call."

" I wasn't," she said. " It was at least half an hour later."

" So if the call did come from this house——"

" It didn't, it didn't ! " she cried. " What evidence have you for suggesting that it did ? "

Justin decided to provide a distraction. " Inspector," he said, " what do you think about the clock on the floor beside Mrs. Allwood, the broken clock ? "

With a certain satisfaction, he saw the exasperation in Turkis's eyes. But before Turkis gave any answer there was a commotion in the hall, a voice was raised in anger, the door was wrenched open and Ben Eagan burst into the kitchen.

He strode straight up to Grace.

" I saw the police here, the ambulance—I thought you'd got hurt."

She lifted her white face to give him a long look. At the sight of the anxiety in his eyes, her own filled with a painful, blurred look of self-mockery, as if she were punishing herself for having allowed the sound of his voice to deceive her, so that for a moment she had expected to see on his face the anxiety, not merely of a kind person, a good friend, but of a lover.

" The body wasn't mine," she said, tight-lipped. " It was a visitor's."

Eagan swung round on Turkis. " What happened ? "

Turkis told him.

At the end of it, Eagan merely looked confused and seemed more excited than before. Walking up and down the kitchen, he exclaimed, " This is fantastical ! This has no sense in it ! " He seemed to be thrown off his balance far more than he had been by the news of Thaine's death, and to have had the usually composed surface of his personality shattered, showing the nervous and explosive nature within.

"Who has anything to gain by this old woman's death? What did she know? What did she see?"

Turkis looked rather pleased about something.

"I believe you've put your finger right on something, Mr. Eagan," he said. "What *did* she see?"

But Eagan was paying no attention to his own question. "There's only one possible explanation of all this," he said. "Someone arranged it to plant suspicion on Grace. There can't be any other explanation. Mrs. Allwood can't have known anything about Arnold's murder, except from what her granddaughter told her, and the girl herself doesn't seem to have known anything of any importance."

"Sure of that, Mr. Eagan?" Turkis asked.

"Anyway, do be quiet, Ben," Grace said harshly.

He quietened down at once. Standing still, he looked at her thoughtfully, looked with a probing and questioning interest, while she looked back at him.

"Anyway," Justin said, raising his voice a little and looking hard at Turkis, "what about the clock?"

Turkis swore under his breath and walked out.

"The clock upsets him," Justin said. "It upsets me too, I feel it should tell us everything we need to know, if only we could understand it. But not understanding it, one's worse confused than if it weren't there—which is what was intended."

He followed Turkis.

Behind him, he heard Grace begin to talk rapidly in a low voice to Eagan.

Turkis was in the sitting-room, from which Mrs. All-wood's body and the broken clock and all signs of disorder, except for a dusting of powder over almost every surface in the room, had been removed.

Justin went up to him and said, "Well, what about the clock, Inspector?"

"The clock," Turkis said, "doesn't mean a thing. Isn't that clear enough?"

"Clear as mud, I'd say," Justin answered.

"Look," Turkis said, simulating patience. "Thaine was killed in a room full of clocks. The clocks had probably nothing whatever to do with his death, but they were there, the bizarre element in the situation. So when the murderer killed Mrs. Allwood, he thought he'd throw in another clock that didn't keep time, just to make it look as if clocks really had something to do with the whole affair. But they hadn't. I'll take my oath on it. If you think too much about clocks, you'll never get anywhere."

" I'm not sure that I agree," Justin said.

" Why not ? "

" I don't know exactly. This afternoon I admitted to someone that I sometimes suffer from intuitions and perhaps that's what's wrong with me. Or perhaps I've noticed something, but don't know what it is."

" Tell me when you find out," Turkis said sarcastically and turned to go.

" Just a minute," Justin said. " What did you mean in there when you suggested Mrs. Allwood must have seen something here."

Turkis paused restively. " You want quite a lot for your money's worth, don't you ? Well, I'll tell you, and then, strange as it may seem, I'm going home to my supper— and I hope no one finds any more bodies till I'm through. Mrs. Allwood came here to see someone. We don't know for certain who it was or why she came and it may be she wasn't even asked to come, but after that telephone conversation this afternoon, just took it into her own head to come. I think myself that that's the most likely thing, because I can't see why anyone here should want to see her. She can't have had any information that could have been dangerous to anyone."

" You think she came out of sheer curiosity ? "

" You can put it like that. And she got here and—well, suppose she saw something through that window, as she came up the path, that she wasn't supposed to see."

" For instance ? "

Turkis replied hesitantly, " This is only a sort of theory, you understand. I haven't had much time yet to think things out. But suppose she saw, say, two people together who aren't supposed to like one another, two people who between them might have decided to do something about Arnold Thaine."

" Two people who dislike one another. . . ." Justin's mind felt clouded, almost deliberately refusing to take in what Turkis was implying.

Turkis turned towards the door. As he went out, he said, " Hasn't it always seemed to you a bit unconvincing, the way Mrs. DeLong's always trying to throw suspicion on Lewis Brillhart, the one person who was safely out of the way when Thaine was killed ? Right from the beginning, I've been waiting till I could find out the truth about those two. And I think perhaps Mrs. Allwood could have told me."

XVI

JUSTIN WANTED to deny it at once. He wanted to tell Turkis that he simply did not understand Grace DeLong and that her explosive dislike of Brillhart was perfectly in keeping with her general character.

Justin could have told Turkis more than that about the situation ; for instance, that an important element in Grace's dislike of Brillhart was almost certainly a belief that she had allowed herself to entertain for a time that Brillhart was strongly attracted by her. Though it seemed that she had not returned this feeling, as she had imagined it to be, her own feelings being all passionately centred on Ben Eagan, the disillusionment that she had suffered when Brillhart had transferred his apparent devotion to Hester had given a bitter wound to Grace's vanity.

Justin believed that the sense of having been deliberately deceived and exploited by Brillhart rankled in her mind quite as much as she had told him, nevertheless that it was her recognition that it had been her own feminine vanity that had really betrayed her into his hands, rather than a purely disinterested sympathy with his troubles, that kept her hatred of him at fever pitch.

But instead of saying any of this, Justin remained silent, almost as if he had accepted Turkis's theory and let Turkis go without replying to him.

For a minute or two afterwards Justin remained standing just where he was, looking rather vacantly before him, though his hands fidgeted with the lighting of a cigarette and with tossing the match towards the hearth, where the fire by now had quite burnt itself out. He was reluctant to go back to Grace and Eagan. Their relationship, which seemed to consist of Grace's suffering an almost continuous pain in the presence of the young man, interspersed with spasms of anger against him, and of Eagan's both shrinking from this and pretending that he did not notice it, roused an intense discomfort in Justin.

He knew that in such a case as this, Grace was hopeless. In fact, it had often seemed to him that she could be counted on always to go looking for the very kind of love that would hurt her most. But whenever he had had the misfortune to have to look on at her, shuddering under the ordeal of it, and finding himself half-contemptuous of her because of it, he had also seemed always to be compelled to feel some of her pain along with her.

At last he returned to the kitchen, where he found that Eagan was making some tea, while Grace sat with her elbows on the table and her head on her hands. Justin had caught no sound of voices as he approached. Both of them looked abstracted, withdrawn from each other into their own thoughts. Eagan glanced at Justin as he came in, but Grace did not stir.

Justin sat down at the table.

"Well," he said, "where do we stand now?"

Neither replied.

He went on, "My own feeling, Grace, is that the time's certainly come for a show down with Eagan. Have you tried anything in that line yet?"

She gave a tired sigh before she answered and closed her eyes. "No, that's what I meant to try this afternoon, then I got knocked on the head. I'm not sure that it seems important any more."

Eagan stopped spooning tea into the teapot.

"Would you like to tell me what you're talking about?" he said.

"About trying to get the truth out of you about one or two things," Justin said.

Eagan put the teapot down on the table. The kettle on the stove was just coming to the boil, but he disregarded it.

"What things?" he asked quietly.

"Mainly about a fire that wasn't alight when you said it was," Justin said.

Grace jerked her chair back from the table with a sudden violent movement.

"That fire," she said, "isn't important. It was in the morning, it can't be important."

"I think it is," Justin said.

She dismissed it with an impatient flick of her hand.

"The letter," she said, "that's the important thing. D'you remember a letter, Ben, a letter that you were in the middle of writing when Justin and I walked in that night?"

The kettle on the stove was filling the air with steam. Ben kept his back turned to it, while the dark eyes in his thin, calm face explored Grace's face with a new wariness in them.

"*That* letter!" he said. "Good God, but I wasn't... It wasn't then... Lord, I wonder what's happened to it. I'd quite forgotten it."

"I've got it," Grace said.

He went on looking at her with a slow change coming over his features, a hardening, a blotting out of all expression. Then he turned away, picked up the kettle and made the tea.

She went on, "I knew you'd forgotten about it. That's why I took it."

"Only for that reason?" he asked in a low voice.

"Yes," she said. "You wouldn't have liked the police to find it, would you?"

"I'm not sure that it would have mattered much," he said.

She gave the table a blow with her hand. "Of course it would have mattered. They'd probably have arrested you by now if they'd found it."

"Explain," he said. But he was not asking for an explanation, he was merely flinging her excuse back in her teeth with rising anger.

"All right," Grace said, small, bright patches of colour appearing over her cheekbones. "I'll tell you the whole thing and you can blame me as much as you like—but I don't blame myself, I'll tell you that in advance. I saw that letter on your table when Justin and I came in that night to tell you about Arnold's death. I could see the letter was to Arnold. Well, I'd heard you quarrel with him the night before in the pub and I'd made two efforts the next day to see him and to try to calm him down. I—I didn't know for certain if there was any truth in these sudden suspicions of his that you were in love with Hester——"

"You know now," Eagan said, low-voiced.

"Yes," Grace said, but seeming to take almost no notice of what Eagan had said. "But I thought the important thing was to prevent another explosion of the kind that Arnold had with Julian Morse. I thought that was important for his sake as well as your own. If a person's always getting involved in affairs of that kind, it doesn't do his reputation any good, and I thought the real truth of the matter was that he'd been worked up by Brillhart with just that object in view. So I went over in the morning—that was when I met you, when you told me about having bust your watch— and I went over in the afternoon, after trying to telephone him several times, about half-past five. But in the morning Arnold wasn't there and in the afternoon he was dead. And your watch was lying on the floor beside him with the strap broken—but that's not what I meant to talk about. I meant to tell you about seeing the letter and deciding I'd better make sure that you'd destroyed it. But you hadn't, it was still there on your desk, where it had been the evening before, with your fountain pen still lying on it, without even its cap put back on it. So then I read the letter and realised that your story of your awfully friendly interview with Arnold couldn't have been true, and——"

"Wait a moment," Justin broke in. "The fountain-pen was still uncapped, you say?"

"Yes," she said, "but——"

He stopped her again by putting a hand on her arm. He spoke to Eagan. "You often do that, I suppose. I mean, you leave your pen lying around like that."

"I dare say I do," Eagan said.

"And in fact you weren't in the middle of writing that letter when Grace and I came."

"That's what I've been trying to tell you," Eagan exclaimed. "No, I wasn't. I was reading, I think. I was feeling so damned relieved that Arnold had quietened down. I'd been rather afraid, you see, that he might try to take things out on Hester, when I didn't think she'd the faintest idea of my state of mind, or that if she had, it wasn't through anything I'd ever done intentionally. But Arnold had almost clapped me on the back when I went in, and told me he was sorry he'd said the things he had, and that he knew who'd been telling the stories about me and that he'd settle his hash for him, and finally that he'd be delighted to mend my watch. So that was that."

"But the letter," Grace said stonily.

"I'd written that the night before, of course," Eagan said.

"And not finished it?"

"No. I'd come in after that scene in the pub, feeling pretty sick, and I'd sat down straight away to write to Arnold. Then, when I'd written a few sentences, I began to feel that perhaps I ought to give the situation more thought, so I stopped writing and after a while I decided that the best thing to do would be to go and talk to Arnold next day. If he was still in the same mood, I'd tell him on the spot that I was leaving, and if he'd recovered, well, perhaps we could sort things out in a better way."

"And you just forgot about the letter and left it lying around?" Grace said.

"Yes."

She sighed again. "I know it's just the sort of thing you do, so it may be true."

"And now suppose you tell us," Justin said, "where you really went in the morning."

Eagan turned his head to look at him. He had quite regained his unconcerned manner, as if he had no real doubt now that he could allay their suspicions. But at Justin's question, he frowned in a provoked and baffled way and began making a nervous little gesture with one hand, rubbing the knuckles against his jawbone.

" I don't understand you," he said.

" You told me earlier that you went over to see Thaine in the morning," Justin said, " that you went to the studio, not knowing what the time was, that you saw the fire hadn't been lit yet, so you concluded that it must be much earlier than you'd thought, and that you then came away."

" Yes," Eagan said. " That's what happened."

" You stick to that, do you ? " Justin said. " You don't want to change the story ? "

" Certainly not."

" Even that detail that the fire hadn't been lit ? "

" No," Eagan said shortly. " It hadn't."

" Oh, Ben, don't be stupid ! " Grace exclaimed. " Of course it had been lit. I was there only a short while after you and there was a fine, glowing fire."

" And Mrs. Thaine says that she'd lit the fire as usual that morning," Justin said, " and made it up just before she left for Wallport."

Eagan looked from one to the other, then deliberately looked away from both of them and drank some tea. His gaze explored the blank wall of the kitchen.

Presently he said, almost idly, " I really don't know what to say."

" Why not tell us where you really went that morning ? " Justin said.

" I can't do that," Eagan said.

" Why not ? " Grace asked eagerly. " Why not trust us, Ben ? "

" I have trusted you," he said.

" Not very far."

" You see, I did go to the Thaines'," he said. " And the fire *was* out."

She sprang to her feet. " This is nonsense. It wasn't. I saw it myself. And Hester knows it too. Not that I can understand why Justin's so set on sorting this out. I don't see why he should think it so important. Arnold wasn't killed till sometime in the afternoon, so I don't know what difference it can make where you really went in the morning. But the more you lie about it, the more important it somehow seems to become. So for God's sake, tell us, Ben—what were you really doing?"

Eagan drank his tea, emptying the cup at one long draught. The tea was still too hot to drink in that way and brought tears to his eyes. Then he got up and went to the door.

"I've told you what I was doing," he said. "I don't see the importance of it either, but if it *is* important, I advise you to believe me."

"I can't believe you," Grace said. "I saw the fire with my own eyes."

He shrugged his shoulders. "I'm sorry. So did I. Or rather, I didn't."

He went out.

Grace sank into her chair and reached for the teapot.

"Well, I don't understand it at all," she said as she refilled her cup, "but that makes me feel it must be important somehow."

"It is," Justin said. "I'm sure it is."

They sat drinking tea for some time, speaking to one another only a little.

Then Grace said wearily, "We've had no dinner. I'd quite forgotten."

"I'm not hungry," Justin said.

"Tell me when you want to go back to your hotel," she said. "I'll drive you back."

"I'm not going back, I'm spending the night here."

She laughed a little. "Without any invitation?"

"With or without. I'm not leaving you alone in this house to-night."

"D'you think he—whoever it was—wants another go at me?"

"I don't know why he should, unless he thinks you saw him."

"I didn't."

"But he might not be sure of that."

" Well, I'm glad you're staying. Will you stay till the end of it, Justin—till the nightmare ends ? "

" I expect so."

" I feel now as if it had been going on for ever," she said. " D'you know what it reminds me of ? It reminds me of the time when Dick died. Those three days when he was ill. When there was no hope and yet they wouldn't come to an end. And it seemed as if there'd never been anything else before them, no marriage, no time with him at all. But afterwards it was the time of his death that faded out of my mind and it was only the other times that I remembered. Until now."

" That's how it usually is," Justin said.

" Yet I always took for granted that I'd marry again sooner or later."

" Well, if you will set your heart on people like Ben Eagan——"

" Oh no, that wasn't the trouble. I think you were the trouble."

He looked at her uneasily.

" Yes," she said, " from the time when Dick first brought you to see me. But I was frightened of it. You weren't in the least like what I thought it was in me to love. I felt I didn't know what might happen to me if I let go of my feelings. So I found Marion for you. I did that on purpose. You didn't know that, did you ? "

He did not answer. Aimlessly, he stirred his tea, watching her with an air of startled concentration. But he knew that what she said of her own feelings about him was true, and that here lay the explanation of his own sense of a debt to her, a debt that could somehow never be paid off.

" But even though I got used to you, you were always there," she went on. " So I went on looking for people whom I could love with the other half of me. People like Dick. Like Ben. And it never worked out. And now tell me something, Justin—about your reason for coming here to see me. Wasn't it to ask me what I knew about Marion, about what happened to her, where she was living ? "

" No," he said, " no."

" I don't believe you."

" I came to see you," he said.

" I don't believe you," she repeated.

" My dear, it's such an old story, the one about Marion and me," he said.

" Old stories have their virtues," she said. " At least one knows how they go. Besides, why don't you think of Marion a little ? "

" She wouldn't even want it."

" She would, I think. You mean something to her that you can't change. But perhaps that doesn't really mean anything much to you. Perhaps underneath you aren't really a very kind person, in spite of all your kindness on the surface. Perhaps you never care very much about anyone."

" Perhaps," he said.

" I've never thought about that before," she said, " but I believe it's the truth. You don't mind much what happens to anyone, you just want to be let alone. And yet you don't like being lonely, I can see that. You know, poor Justin, I believe you're just as much of a mess as I am."

" I don't doubt it."

" No, you probably don't. You wouldn't deceive yourself. Yet I dare say you strike most people as knowing just what you want in life."

" Who does really ? "

" Some people. Arnold did."

" What did he want—clocks ? "

" Clocks and Hester."

" Did he really want Hester ? "

" He wanted a beautiful and unusual woman in his house, to move beautifully and dress beautifully, among his beautiful belongings."

" Which reminds me. . . ." Justin pushed his chair back and began to walk up and down the room, anxious to break the tension that had grown during the last few minutes between Grace and himself. " When she turned all Thaine's furniture out of her sitting-room and brought in all that Victorian stuff, what did Thaine make of it ? And what did you make of it ? "

Grace laughed oddly, perhaps a little spitefully, as if she had recognised the intention behind the turn that he had given to the conversation.

" But it wasn't Hester who turned Arnold's furniture out, it was Arnold himself," she said.

" Brillhart told me it was Hester."

" There, you see—Brillhart," she said. " Haven't I told you not to believe anything he says ? "

" Brillhart's suggestion was that she'd done it because she'd heard and believed the stories circulating about Arnold. And I'm not sure Brillhart wasn't even suggesting that she might have been circulating the stories herself—though when I asked him if that was what he meant, he denied it."

" Of course, he's wonderful at denying things. Didn't you gather that from Julian Morse ? "

" Yes. All the same, why should Arnold suddenly move all his furniture out of the drawing-room ? "

" Oh, I know all about that. It was simply because he decided that his furniture didn't suit Hester. Someone so slender and quiet, with that slightly broken-lily touch that Hester has, needed a Victorian background, he thought. He recognised that she was quite the rarest piece of furniture in his house, so he decided to provide an appropriate décor."

" And Hester was angry ? "

" Of course. Wouldn't you have been ? "

" She admired his work, then ? "

" Yes, and I think that to begin with she thought she was going to play some part in connection with it, help with the business side or something. But he didn't let that idea last long."

Justin gave a stretch and then a yawn.

" D'you know, I've taken a great dislike to Arnold Thaine during the last two days," he said. " I'm glad it wasn't my misfortune to know him."

" You wouldn't have disliked him if you'd known him," Grace said. " You'd have accepted him for what he was, like the rest of us."

" One person didn't," Justin said. " His spell didn't work on everyone."

"I'm not sure of that. Perhaps he was killed because the spell worked too strongly. After all, envy and hatred can come out of an excessive admiration, can't they?"

"You're still thinking of Brillhart. That's so foolish, Grace."

"I can't help it," she said.

"It could be dangerous too."

"What d'you mean?"

For a moment he considered telling her of Turkis's suspicion that her loathing of Brillhart was not as violent as it seemed. But he decided that she could wait to hear this troubling piece of information until after a night's sleep. Once more changing the subject he asked her if she had any sleeping pills in the house and advised her, if she had, to take one.

She shook her head and said, "Don't worry, I'll sleep."

Soon afterwards she went up to bed.

Justin went to the sitting-room and because the fire had gone out and the room become quite cold, he plugged in an electric fire that he found in a corner and switched it on. The room felt oppressive and eerie, full of the presence of the woman who had died in it, yet Justin felt that he must spend the night there. It was his obligation, he felt, a part of his irredeemable debt, to watch over Grace that night, to see that the killer did not return to the house.

Making up his mind to this, he reflected on Grace's accusation that there was very little real kindness in him, very little real care for other people. It was true enough, probably. He took his obligations seriously, those imposed on him by his intelligence and by a rather sensitive sense of guilt, but perhaps some warmth was lacking, some power to identify himself with others, of which he knew very little.

The hours of the night went by achingly, exhaustingly. He read for most of the time. But sometimes his mind wandered, as it had not done for many years, to the image of Marion Garston. It was almost as painful to let it do this as to remove a blood-soaked bandage from a dried wound. Again and again his imagination shrank from it. But each time, involuntarily, it started exploring the sore spot again. Perhaps the place had not really healed as well as he had supposed. There might be something in it that he ought to examine and cleanse before applying a new dressing of forgetfulness. And perhaps forgetfulness was not the right treatment. Perhaps the courage of a clearer memory would serve him better. The memory of something passionate and absorbingly beautiful in its pain and long drawn out frustration.

But alongside his thoughts of Marion ran a nagging and recurrent question. Why did Eagan insist on lying about visiting the Thaines' house on the morning of the day on which Thaine had been murdered? Why should he insist on saying that he had been there, when obviously he had not? What had he to conceal, unless it was that in spite of all his denials that Hester Thaine had known anything of his feelings for her before her husband's death, he had been meeting her secretly?

The image of Hester Thaine began to trouble Justin's tired mind. It was the image of a woman who perhaps had more motive than anyone else to wish her husband dead and who perhaps had never gone to a cinema in Wallport, but had known how to enter her own home unobserved by the old man in the cottage and shoot her husband while he sat amidst his clocks. His valuable, unreliable clocks, to which he allowed the full liberty of their imperfections, their faulty mechanisms.

XVII

By the morning Justin knew what he had to do next. He had to take another look at Arnold Thaine's studio.

He could not have said exactly what it was that he hoped to find there, but he had a strong feeling that it was important for him to see that room once more, with its strange furnishing of ticking clocks, and to see it, if possible by himself, so that he could let his imagination work without interruption on the scene of the crime.

Soon after it was light, he tiptoed to the bathroom and washed, then went to the kitchen and made himself some coffee, then slipped quietly out of doors and set off to the Thaines' house.

The cold air invigorated him. There was a faint white coating of frost on the ground and a light, low mist among the trees. He met one man, plodding along the road to work, but except for him, the country roads were deserted. In some high tree-tops some crows sat motionless. Somewhere in the distance a dog barked.

Justin reached the Thaines' gate and pushed it open.

A feeling came to him at once that now he must move quietly, a feeling of furtiveness, of being about to do things which he did not want observed. A little surprised at himself, he realised that he was walking softly on the grass border of the path instead of on the gravel. But this was going farther in attempting to remain unseen than he really intended and he stepped on to the path again.

At most, if he should be observed by anyone, particularly by the old man at his bedroom window in the cottage, he hoped that he would appear like someone who was anxious not to disturb others at that early hour, rather than as someone with a fear of being seen.

Reaching the house, he walked round it to the studio at the back. He was prepared for the studio to be locked and for it to be necessary to limit his inspection of the room to a look through the window. But since it was not only the room itself that he wanted to see, but the approach to it from all parts of the garden, he was not much put out by this thought. However, when he reached the studio, the door opened with only a touch on the handle. Almost, he thought as he went in, it was as if Hester Thaine were inviting someone to come and steal her husband's valuable clocks, to take them out of her life, to let her forget that they had ever existed.

As soon as he was inside and had closed the door, he felt a change in the room. He felt it even before he had looked round. When he did look round and could see no change at all there, except that Thaine's dead body was gone, he thought at first that his sense of some important alteration having been made was deceptive, was almost superstitious and merely an expression of his knowledge that death had come and gone from the room. But then he realised that his sense of change was perfectly accurate, only that it was his ears and not his eyes that had told him of it. There was far less sound in the room than had been there before. One by one, as they ran down and were left unwound, the clocks had been stopping.

For some reason, the discovery chilled him. It was like a second death in the room. There was so little sound there now that it resolved itself into several separately audible rhythms of ticking, and even while he stood there listening, one of these, that had been like an incredibly slow pulse, gradually losing all vigour, made a last faint rattling sound and stopped. Justin tried to resist the feeling that came to him that the clock had just gasped out its life.

He began to wander round the room, not touching anything, not knowing what he hoped to find. So far as he could tell, all had been left precisely as it had been on the evening of the crime. Thaine's papers still lay spread out over the big table. Even Ben Eagan's watch with the broken strap was still there. The ashes in the fireplace had not been disturbed. But then Justin realised that the clock with the dangling weights, that had hung on the wall over the fireplace, was gone.

From the doorway a voice spoke, " Good morning, Mr. Emery."

He swung round, startled and even for an instant, afraid. There was no apparent reason why he should fear anything. Hester Thaine stood there, her arms spread out and each hand holding on to a side of the doorway. It was almost the position in which he remembered seeing her first, when it had looked as if she had needed the support of the doorposts to keep her from falling. She was dressed in a grey knitted jersey and grey tweed skirt and her fair hair was loose on her shoulders ; she looked far younger than he had ever seen her look before, more human, less of a shadow.

"You're very early," she said. "Would you like some breakfast?"

He smiled. "Don't I even have to apologise for being here?"

"I know why you're here," she said, "and it doesn't call for an apology."

She came farther into the room, looking round her almost as if the place were unfamiliar to her.

"D'you know I haven't been in here since I found Arnold dead? Does that seem to you very unnatural?"

"You always hated it, didn't you?" Justin said.

"Yes, I hated it. Not at first. At first I just thought it a rather fascinating hobby of Arnold's. But by degrees it came to mean something quite different to me. It came to stand for the whole horrible mistake I'd made in marrying him." She stood still, her eyes raised to the empty space on the wall where the lantern-clock had hung. "One-five," she muttered. "That's what that clock said. In my mind that's come to stand for a moment outside of time. I hope we never find out what the real time was."

"I think we will find out," Justin said.

"Oh, I hope not," she said softly.

"Don't you want to know who killed your husband?" he asked, not censoriously but curiously.

"No, I'd far sooner never know." She turned her head to look into Justin's face. "Do they shock you, these things I'm saying?"

He shrugged slightly, watching her interestedly and non-committally.

She laid a hand on the back of a chair and sat down on it sideways, folding her arms on the back.

"At first I wanted to know it, more than I've ever wanted to know anything," she said. "But I've gone a long distance during the last few days. I'm thinking very differently. I think I'm almost a different person."

He shook his head. "No, that never happens so fast."

She contradicted him with a quick, emphatic nod.

"Yes, sometimes. I know it means it was all there in one beforehand, and that all that's happened is that one's become aware of it. But that awareness alone is so much—it's such a difference. It's a new kind of air to breathe."

"You know, you sound almost happy," he said thoughtfully.

She flushed. "You may be quite right. At least I think I've stopped being positively unhappy, which I have been for a long time. And I realise that must sound as if I'm utterly callous, but I'm not that. I'm not without a great sorrow for Arnold. But it's not the centre of my life and at first I thought it was."

"Why did you marry him?" he asked.

"Oh, love—no other reason," she said. "I was a bad case of it. I thought I knew the answer to the whole problem of human happiness, that it had come to me miraculously without any effort on my part and that it was mine for ever. I knew, of course, that it wasn't like that for other people, but for me I was sure it was. And now I'm beginning to think that Arnold, as a person, hardly entered into my consciousness at all."

"I wonder," Justin said, "what's really taught you such a lot so quickly."

"Ah, you know," she said, "or I shouldn't be talking like this at all. If I didn't think that you already know nearly all that's been happening to me, I shouldn't say a word."

"But I know very little of you," he said.

"There's no need to pretend," she answered. "I don't mind your knowing about Ben and me. Though that isn't the whole of it, naturally."

"No," he said. "But what do you intend to do about it?"

"Oh, we'll marry," she said. "But not yet, not for a good while."

"And you'll stay here?"

"No," she said, "never. Does that surprise you?"

"In a way. Yet in your place, I'd certainly go away."

"A long way away," she said. "As far as possible. It's not only Arnold's death I want to leave behind, you know, but my life with him, my own mistakes and my own—my own guilt."

He raised his eyebrows.

"Yes," she said. "Don't think I'm blaming Arnold because I wasn't happy. I think that neither of us was ever able to think of the other as a real person. I think I starved him of real human feeling as much as he did me. I thought of him as the great artist to whom everything I had and was must be sacrificed. I think I'd have insisted on making the sacrifice even if he hadn't expected it. And that's a rather wicked thing to do to a person, isn't it?"

"It sounds like it," Justin said, "if what you say is true. But I'm inclined to think that perhaps it isn't."

"It is," she said.

"But it all sounds a little too simple. I think I'd wait a while before trying to explain the whole of your marriage to yourself."

She looked a little put out. "D'you mind my talking to you like this?"

"Of course not."

"The things come out of me, whether I want them to or not. But I have to keep them back when Ben's there. It seems to hurt him horribly if I talk of Arnold at all."

"So you're already making that sacrifice to Ben," Justin said.

"I don't call that a sacrifice."

"Did you call the other things sacrifices, the things you did for your husband, at the beginning?"

She looked at him blankly for a moment, then laughed.

"No, oh no, of course not. So you don't think I can change my spots."

"So few people ever do."

"But if one has help . . . Ben's an unusual person, you know. He doesn't look it, but there's a great deal of strength in him really, if he's given the chance to show it. I think that's partly why I attracted him—that I really am a very helpless person and he feels that that strength of his can be used on my account. Or does all that strike you as stupid too? Am I making it all too simple again?"

"Does it matter much, even if you are? And what will Ben do when you leave here? Will he stick to the same kind of work?"

"Of course. He must. He's every bit as gifted as Arnold."

"And Brillhart?"

She looked troubled. "I wish I knew what to make of him. It was he who advised me straight away to get rid of the whole place here. But he won't go with us. He refuses to work for me. He even refuses any sort of help from me, except the salary that Arnold would have owed him for the next three months. And with his wife to look after, I know that won't go far. I'm very worried. I think he's been so upset by Grace's attitude that he thinks mine must really be the same and he simply wants to get away from us all. I've told him my feelings aren't like hers at all, that I've always liked and believed in him and that I'm certain he had nothing to do with spreading the stories about Arnold. But he's a very sensitive and emotional little man and I think he feels so terribly hurt about everything that he wants to get away from us all as soon as he can."

"When I saw him first," Justin said, "I thought he was in love with you."

She smiled, shaking her head. "No, that's just his manner. It doesn't mean a thing."

"And if he didn't spread the stories, who did?"

She answered without hesitation, "Rhona and Julian Morse."

He showed his dissatisfaction with the suggestion by frowning out of the window.

"Don't you agree?" Hester asked, with slightly more anxiety in her voice than he had expected.

"No, I'm afraid I don't," he said. "I think Brillhart did spread those stories. At first I kept an open mind about it, because Grace's antagonism to him seemed so exaggerated. But I spent most of last night awake, trying to piece things together, and I can't come to any conclusion but that Brillhart did set the slander going."

"But why—why?" she exclaimed. "He'd nothing to gain by it. It could only do him damage in the end."

"So far as there was anything calculated in his mind," Justin said, "he may have thought that by damaging Morse and then Eagan in your husband's eyes, by making him believe that they'd been slandering him, he himself had a chance to step into their shoes."

"But where would have been the sense in that? Arnold paid Lewis much more than he did either of the others. After all, Lewis was a competent and experienced craftsman, he could direct other men and do beautiful work himself. The other two were just learners."

"I don't myself think that any of that is particularly important," Justin said. "I think he invented and spread the stories simply because he couldn't stop himself. Arnold Thaine was a man who had some greatness about him, he was big physically, he was a powerful personality. In other words, he was something worth destroying, and that is something that some people can't resist. Brillhart could begin by setting him up on a pedestal, then have all the more satisfaction in bringing him down. It's a common enough type of mind, you know."

She gave a slight shiver. "I can't really believe it. He's always been so kind to me. He's almost the kindest person I've known. I think you must have been listening too much to Grace."

"I don't think so." Justin did not want to tell her that some of Brillhart's curious negative slanders, spread by contradiction, had even implicated her. "But that doesn't mean that he was your husband's murderer, you know. In fact, we're certain that he wasn't. Personally, I don't feel at all sure that the stories had anything whatever to do with the murder. Or at the most, I'd say, they only provided the climate in which the murder happened."

"And we're still no nearer than we were to clearing the thing up?"

"It seems not."

She bent her head, resting her cheek on the arm that was crooked on the back of the chair. As she stared emptily before her, Justin, waiting to see if she had any more to say to him, noticed the soft, loose hair curving on her neck and the brittle grace of her body, even in the odd, uncomfortable posture that she had taken up on the wooden chair.

He had thought of her a great deal during the night before, thought of her with growing doubt and suspicion, and it had seemed to him that there were a number of things about her that he must find out with all speed. But these thoughts, these questions, had been driven confusedly out of his mind by the unexpected openness with which she had spoken to him.

After a silence, she lifted her head and then, as if her limbs had become stiff and weary while she had been sitting there, pushed herself up awkwardly from the chair.

As soon as she moved, Justin remembered one of the things that he had meant to ask her.

" Mrs. Thaine . . ."

She interrupted him. " You haven't had breakfast, have you ? "

" No," he said, " but there's something I want to ask——"

" Questions," she said, " always questions."

" Yes. It can't be helped. This is an important one."

" If it's about that poor woman yesterday . . ."

" No." With a start he realised that this was the first that either of them had said of Mrs. Allwood, and that if Hester herself had not mentioned her, he might have remained uncertain if she had even heard of the second murder. " No, it's about Ben Eagan. I want to know— and it *is* important—if you saw him on Saturday morning before you left for Wallport."

She looked so surprised and puzzled that it was easy to assume that there was no possibility of her having met Eagan on the Saturday morning. But she took so long to reply that it seemed to Justin that she was giving herself a suspicious amount of time in which to decide on her answer.

At last she simply said, " No."

" You'll stick to that ? "

" Yes, certainly. Why ? "

" Because of some things that Eagan said about a visit here that morning. I don't believe he ever came here at all. And so I want to know what he was really doing."

" I don't know," she said. " I haven't any idea."

" You didn't see him ? "

" No."

" And you can't suggest why he should want it to be thought that he did come here that morning, if he didn't ? "

There was a deepening look of alarm on her face.

" No—no, I can't. And I don't see why you call it important. I don't see how it can be."

" I don't either, really," he said, in a tone of apology. " But it's the one quite incomprehensible lie that's been told me during the last two days. I've heard a great many others, but they've either been explained away as misunderstandings or the reason for them has become fairly apparent. All Grace's lies, for instance—and she's told a great many— they hang together in a form I can understand. But this lie of Eagan's, that he sticks to so stubbornly—it's so senseless, it has to mean something."

She turned towards the door.

" Perhaps that's all it is, just senseless."

" But he isn't a fool. If he'd merely blundered in the first place, he could have retracted it later. He's had plenty of opportunity to do that."

" Well, I know nothing about it," she said in a tone of finality and went out into the garden.

Justin followed her. The sun was higher in the sky now and the light frost was already fading into a moisture on the grass. There was a pleasant, wintry glitter in the air. Justin and Hester walked towards the house. He realised that he had failed to do the main thing for which he had come, which had been to take a careful look at the garden and the possible approaches to the studio. But he might be able to do that later. The thought of breakfast had become very attractive to him and he did not attempt to linger.

But then something caught his eye and he stopped abruptly.

Hester paused and looked at him questioningly, saw where he was looking and laughed.

" Oh, that—it's funny, isn't it ? And it's the only clock in the place that's right. I believe it almost irked Arnold that it wouldn't go wrong unless he tampered with it, which of course would have been going too far."

Side by side, they walked towards the old sun-dial on the lawn.

Justin could not have told just then why the sight of it so excited him. He only knew that, as soon as he saw it, he was looking at something that was of the greatest importance, something that had been overlooked until then, but which now, on the spot, might yield up to him a secret that would resolve all his perplexities.

The only clock in the place that was right. . . .

He stopped beside it, looking down at the metal dial. It was of a common type, with two circles of figures around it and some words printed at the outer edge. The metal was worn and the words were almost obscured, but with the tip of a finger he traced them out, speaking them aloud as he did so.

" Gather ye rosebuds while ye may, olde tyme is still a-flying."

Hester laughed and said, " It's rather trite."

" ' Olde tyme . . .' " Justin's voice suddenly became hoarse and he stopped.

He saw it all now, the whole thing. It had all been in his mind since the night before, but the pieces had not fitted together into any pattern that had meant anything to him until this moment when he had seen the sun-dial, the only clock in the place that, silently, had been telling the truth.

But the pattern was so hideous, so vile, that he hardly dared to think of it.

Yet now all the pieces fitted into it. Even Ben Eagan's lie about his visit to the Thaines' house fitted into it, or rather, Justin saw now that it had not been a lie at all.

Eagan had been telling the truth when he said that the fire had been out.

XVIII

HESTER'S FACE grew puzzled, then apprehensive, as she saw the change of expression on Justin's.

"Well, shall we go in?" she said with nervous impatience, as if she felt it an urgent matter to interrupt his train of thought.

"Yes," he said, "of course." But he did not move from the sun-dial. It held him fascinated.

From the doorway of the house a voice called to them, "Hester! Emery!"

They both turned and saw Brillhart, his big eyes blazing with excitement, hurrying towards them. His face was flushed and there were drops of sweat on his forehead.

"They've arrested Grace!" He seemed to make an effort to say it calmly, but it came out falsetto.

"No, no," Hester said quickly, "that's not possible!" She turned on Justin. "It isn't possible, is it?"

He lifted his eyes to hers, but had difficulty in taking in what she was saying. He even had difficulty in seeing her properly. His thoughts kept on relentlessly along their new-found path.

In a shocked voice, she said, "You almost look as if you'd been expecting it."

"So I have—in a way—since yesterday," he said, and he could hear the odd, flat sound of indifference in his own voice. Trying to pull himself together, to speak as they expected him to speak, he added, "I rather thought they'd do something of the sort."

"But Grace——!" Brillhart cried, almost dancing up and down in his excitement. "There isn't a particle of sense in it, no reason, no probability. And I'd taken that man Turkis for a man of some intelligence."

"He is," Justin said sombrely. "Even more than I'd realised. He's so nearly right."

" I don't understand you," Hester said, her voice becoming very cold. " As Lewis says, there's not a grain of sense in arresting Grace. She had no motive of any kind for murdering Arnold."

" I suppose it's because Mrs. Allwood was killed in her house," Brillhart said. " But she was knocked out herself, wasn't she. Isn't that the truth, Emery ? You were there. Isn't it true what Ben told me, that she'd been knocked out herself ? "

" Yes, quite true," Justin said.

" Then why do the police go and make fools of themselves by arresting her ? " Brillhart went on. " Do they doubt that the attack was real ? "

" It certainly looks as if they do," Justin said.

" But it's nonsense, nonsense ! " Brillhart cried. " Anyone could have come and gone from that house and attacked both the women."

" It's the motive that's beyond me," Hester said. " They must know that Grace had no motive for killing Arnold."

" Your husband's death was an accident," Justin began. Then he frowned at himself for what he had said. " No, that isn't what I mean. But there was something accidental in it. That it was Arnold Thaine who was killed—that was to some extent accidental."

" I don't understand you." There was frigid anger in Hester's voice, as if she found something unspeakably shocking in Justin's failure at this moment to champion Grace's innocence.

" Nor do I, it's absurd, it's the wildest absurdity," Brillhart said. " Was the old woman's death also an accident ? Is that how you explain away the utter lack of motive, so far as Grace is concerned."

" That wouldn't be so difficult to understand," Hester said, " if one could understand Arnold's murder. Mrs. Allwood must have known something that made her dangerous. I suppose her granddaughter told her something, possibly not realising its meaning. But Arnold . . ."

" I think, you know, I'll go and have a talk with Turkis," Justin said.

"Now?" Brillhart asked. "Straight away? I'll drive you over, if you like. That is—that is, if you're going because you think you can help Grace in some way."

Justin gave him a long, serious look. "You seem very anxious to return good for evil."

"There's no evil in Grace," Brillhart said. "She liked me for a time, then she took a dislike to me, that's all. But while she liked me, she did more to help me than anyone I've ever known. That's all I can think of now. Well, shall I drive you into Archersfield?"

"Thanks," Justin said. "I'd be grateful if you would."

"I hope it's to help Grace you're going," Hester said, "not the opposite."

She turned and went quickly into the house.

"She's awfully upset," Brillhart said. "She doesn't believe it was Grace any more than I do."

"But I don't think it's really that that's upsetting her," Justin said. "I'm afraid it was I who did that, by asking her some questions about Ben and a fire that was out. I'm very sorry about it, because, as it turns out, the questions were quite unnecessary."

Brillhart gave a wondering shake of his head. "I don't understand you. There's something queer about you this morning."

"I feel queer," Justin said. "However, let's go."

Brillhart repeated the shake of his head, then led the way round the house and out to the road, where he had left his car.

At first, on their way to Archersfield, he and Justin did not talk much. Brillhart had a small, old, ramshackle car, which he handled in an uncertain and excitable fashion, which resulted in Justin's having the feeling that they might bounce off the road at any moment, but at least kept the attention of Brillhart so occupied that Justin, for a short time, could plan what he meant to say to Turkis.

But presently Brillhart confided in him, "Driving always does me good. It relieves me when I get into a state of unbearable tension. If I had a good car, I should probably be a very fast and dangerous driver, just to calm my own nerves. I see no prospect of ever owning a good car, so there's nothing to worry about."

"Have you any plans for the future?" Justin asked.

"Just to look for a job," Brillhart said.

"And will that be easy?"

"A job of some sort, yes. But one quite like this . . ." Brillhart shrugged.

"Yet it was you, Mrs. Thaine told me," Justin said, "who advised her to shut things down here and move away."

"She told you that? Well, it's quite true, I did. I told her so that first evening, when I stayed on with her after you and Grace had gone. It's quite obvious to me that it's the best thing for her to do. After all, if she stayed on and if after a time she married Ben and he stepped into Arnold's shoes in the business, there'd never be any end to the rumours about them and that would have made life hell for them both."

"Even if the murderer had been caught?"

Brillhart hesitated for a moment, then said in a flat tone, "Do you really expect that to happen, Emery?"

"Why, yes, I think it will," Justin said. "And suppose it wasn't Ben who took over control in the business, but you . . ."

"I thought of that, naturally," Brillhart said. "One always thinks of oneself, even if one afterwards pretends one hasn't. But things like that just don't happen to me. Besides—well, in a way, I don't want to stay."

"Even if the next job isn't what it might be?"

"Yes. Next time I mean to be very careful to remain on as impersonal a footing with everyone connected with the job as I can. Emotions and work don't go well together. With Hester, for instance—I'll tell you this frankly—she means a lot too much to me for my own peace of mind. It's going to hurt like hell, but it'll be best for me in the long run, if I get away from her. With the way things are in my life, I can't have entanglements with women, even if, for a moment, she'd think of me with anything more than the kind, quiet sympathy she's always shown. So I wasn't being altogether unselfish when I said it'd be best for her to end things here—because, if she had decided to stay on, I'd at least have had to stay on and help her over the beginning. And among other things, I'd like to get away from Grace—a long way away. I expect you can understand that. But now there's something I want to ask you, Emery."

"Yes?"

"You talked about Arnold's death having been accidental. What on earth did you mean by that?"

Justin stared sightlessly down the road ahead of him, reminding himself to be careful not to say too much yet.

"It was simply a silly thing to say," he said.

"But you meant something by it."

"Yes."

"Of course, if you don't want to tell me . . ."

"Wait a little," Justin said. "I'll tell you more later."

"When you've talked with Turkis?"

Justin nodded.

"All right, I won't bother you any further."

Looking offended, Brillhart concentrated once more on his erratic driving, which resulted, Justin thought, in the car curvetting and prancing worse than ever.

When they reached the police station in Archersfield, Brillhart asked Justin if he would like him to wait for him in the car, but Justin said, "No, come in with me. You may be able to help."

"But I don't know what you want to say to Turkis."

"You'll soon see what I'm trying to get at."

"All right then." Muttering something else under his breath, Brillhart followed Justin into the police station and stood behind him, looking restless and unsure of himself, while Justin asked the man at the desk for Inspector Turkis.

They were taken into a small, bare office which was empty when they went into it, but in a minute or two Turkis joined them, coming in hurriedly and abstractedly and failing, Justin noted, to look him in the eye, as if the mere sight of Justin there filled him with embarrassment.

"So you've heard already," Turkis said.

"Yes," Justin said, "but that isn't what I came to talk about exactly. I wanted to ask you something about telephone calls. I think you said yesterday that calls between Archersfield and Wallport can be traced."

"Yes, of course. And if it's the call that brought Mrs. Allwood over here yesterday afternoon that you want to know about, I can only tell you that it was made from a call-box here in Archersfield, not from Mrs. DeLong's house."

"Ah, I was sure of that," Justin said. "However, I don't suppose you ever imagined that Mrs. DeLong had made that call."

"No, I didn't, as a matter of fact."

"You thought it was made by her accomplice, her partner in murder."

"Yes, though why they should have wanted to see Mrs. Allwood, I don't know yet. And Miss Allwood can't tell us anything about it, nor can the girl at the switchboard in the hotel. All that Miss Allwood knows is that her grand-mother suddenly said she must go to Archersfield to see someone who had just called her and that she ordered out the car and went."

"And this accomplice——"

Brillhart broke in, "What is this about an accomplice? Where has this idea come from? What makes you think that two people were involved?"

"But of course two people were involved," Justin said. "You don't think Grace knocked herself out by herself, do you? At the most, if the inspector's right that she, the woman in brown, murdered Thaine, she must have allowed her accomplice to knock her out, so as to provide her with a bulletproof alibi, just as she—if the inspector's right—murdered Thaine when her partner had an equally sound alibi."

Looking a little surprised, Turkis nodded. "Yes, that's right."

A look of the deepest incredulity had appeared in Brillhart's bulging eyes. His face had flushed, as it usually did in moments of intense excitement.

" But how can you prove—— ? " he began.

Justin interrupted, " All the same, Inspector, it wasn't that telephone call that I wanted to ask you about, but another. You know that when I recognised Miss Allwood and followed her in the bus to Wallport, she made a call from a telephone box to her fiancé in London, a call that didn't get through, so that she had to call him again later from the hotel ? "

" Yes," Turkis said, " she told me about that."

" And have you traced that call ? "

" No, I——" Turkis checked himself and a quick frown wrinkled his forehead.

" I should," Justin said, " I really should, because I don't think that that call was made to London at all. I think it was made to Archersfield, to Mr. Brillhart's number, and if only the operator had been listening in to the call, I think she'd be able to tell you that Miss Allwood told Brillhart that he must get rid of his dog immediately, before its liking for her betrayed the fact that she was well acquainted with him."

Brillhart gave a gasp, then cried out angrily. The flush disappeared from his face, leaving it a yellowish grey.

" Inspector," he cried, " are you going to listen to any more of this ? You know that this man is a friend of Mrs. DeLong's, that he'll do anything, say anything to drag her to safety at the expense of anyone else—even of that poor girl in Wallport, whom we all know had never seen Arnold Thaine in her life ? "

Turkis did not even glance towards him. He still frowned and his eyes had become hard, but they were acutely interested.

" Go on," he said to Justin.

" What Mr. Brillhart says is perfectly correct," Justin said. " Miss Allwood had never seen Arnold Thaine in her life. She had no connection with him of any kind. He meant nothing to her whatever. Yet all the same, when she went to see him, she took a gun along with her and shot him dead."

Brillhart had started to tremble violently.

"Are you mad?" he shouted at Justin in a high, strange voice.

"No," Justin said, "and neither are you, that's the horror of it. You're a sane, far-seeing, calculating man who knows just what you want and how to get it."

"Just a minute, Emery," Turkis said. "You said yourself that Miss Allwood had no connection with Thaine."

"And it's true, it's true," Justin said. "That's the cleverness of it and the frightfulness of it. And when her grandmother was killed, which was the murder that really counted, the one with which she really had some connection, the one that would have left her and her partner rich, if they could have got away with it, she was miles away from the spot, having tea with me. Oh yes, she was, she definitely was; she has a perfect alibi for her grandmother's murder. And you were perfectly right, Inspector, that these murders were done by two people, each with an alibi arranged for the time of the murder that might be traced to him, only you got one of the people wrong when you arrested Mrs. DeLong."

There was a short silence in the room. It was broken only by the sound of Brillhart's deep breathing, but his lips were clamped shut, as if in a struggle with himself to hold back the words that were ready to pour out.

Then Turkis said, "And how did you arrive at this theory, Mr. Emery?"

"Guesswork, of course," Justin said. "But you'll see that it all fits together. Checking on such things as that telephone call and whether or not the gun that she used to kill Thaine is still in Miss Allwood's possession, or whether its purchase can be traced to her or Brillhart, I leave to you."

"Guesswork, guesswork," Brillhart muttered.

"Yes, it's guesswork, for instance," Justin said, "that Miss Allwood and Brillhart got to know one another in India during the war. All the same, it's something you might check up on too. Mrs. DeLong told me that Brillhart was fond of relating his war experiences and that among his other stories about himself was one of how he'd been dropped by parachute behind the Japanese lines. Well, I don't think he'd have risked that unless he could fill in a little background about life in the East, and that it wasn't improbable, therefore, that he'd at least got as far as India. However, where they met in the first place isn't perhaps so very important. The important thing is that they've met more recently, and that's something that I ought to have realised as soon as I learnt a little about the nature of Brillhart's dog. Everyone told me the same thing about the dog, that he was a bad-tempered beast who hated all strangers. Yet the very first time I saw him, in the square, on my first morning in Archersfield, he was showing the greatest pleasure at seeing Miss Allwood. In most dogs of a normally friendly disposition that wouldn't have meant anything, but with this dog it could only mean that he and she were already friends. And he followed her about for the rest of the day, until she shut him up in the Thaines' house. And it was because she saw him in the square the next day and was afraid that he would rush up to her, that she ran for the bus. And when I ran after her and jumped on the bus too, Brillhart ran after me, shouting, as a warning to her that she was being followed."

"Go on," Turkis said. "This is getting interesting."

"It is," Justin agreed. "You see, that moment when I saw her in the square in the morning really told me all I needed to know. There she stood in the sunshine in her red coat, with the dog wagging his tail at her . . ."

"Why did she wear a red coat?" Turkis said. "Almost any other colour would have been less conspicuous."

"I think—I think Brillhart insisted on it," Justin said. "It was part of the price he asked for murdering her grandmother, that she should make herself conspicuous in Archersfield that day. All the same, it wasn't the red coat, or even the dog, that betrayed her that morning. It was the sun. If the sun hadn't shone at just that moment when she got down from the bus, I doubt if I'd know yet who committed the murder. And I only realised that this morning when I was looking at a sundial in Arnold Thaine's garden. The sundial made me remember those few minutes of sunshine during the morning of a day when it had rained and rained—and suddenly I understood why a man should swear that a fire had been out when in fact it had undoubtedly been alight. That had seemed such a pointless lie—if it *was* a lie—that it had come to seem important. But the truth is that it wasn't a lie at all. Eagan had simply described what he saw."

"I don't follow you now," Turkis said. "What has the sun got to do with it?"

"Well, it just happened that on the Saturday morning, when Miss Allwood got down from the bus and the sun shone and the dog wagged its tail at her, and I, hurrying to the bus, noticed that the time was just eleven-twenty, Ben Eagan was standing at the window of Thaine's study, looking in. And because the sun was shining so brightly at that moment, two things happened. He saw the time clearly on the face of the clock hanging over the fireplace, and he thought that there was no fire in the grate. You've noticed that yourself, I'm sure—when the sun shines brightly enough directly on to an open fire, the glow of the fire disappears and it looks as if there were nothing there but ash. There's even a common superstition, which makes some people actually draw the curtains when the sun shines on to a fire, that the sun puts the fire out. So Ben Eagan looked into the room and he thought that the fire was out and that's what he told me later, thereby convincing me that he was lying about ever having been to the studio at all in the morning and that it was no good relying on anything he might tell me about the time he saw on the clock. But in fact, if you believe what he said, you can work out the exact time when a bullet was shot into that clock, and that happens to have been the time when Miss Allwood was in the studio."

"But the motive," Turkis said. "What was her motive for shooting Thaine? What did she or Brillhart stand to gain by shooting Thaine?"

"Nothing," Justin said. "Nothing at all. Brillhart even stood to lose. It's true that Thaine had just discovered that Brillhart was the person who'd been spreading slanderous stories about him and so Brillhart was liable to lose his job.

But it's unlikely that Brillhart knew about that when he set off for London that morning to establish his alibi. Probably he imagined his slanders would never catch up with him. And with Thaine's death he was almost certain to lose his job anyhow. This morning, indeed, he took the trouble to let us know that he'd been persuading Hester Thaine to close down her husband's workshops, so that it should be perfectly clear that no benefit of any kind could come to him from Thaine's death."

"But then why murder Thaine at all ? " Turkis asked.

Brillhart exploded, "Yes, in heaven's name, even if a word of this were true, why should I murder Arnold ? Not one thing you've said makes sense of that."

"But it does," Justin said heavily and a sudden feeling of acute distaste for himself, his knowledge and the part he was playing overcame him and made him for a moment lose the thread of his thoughts. But a flicker of scepticism in Turkis's eyes made him pull himself together. "Oh, it does," he said. "That's the really horrible part of it all, the part that it sickens one to think about. I said to Brillhart and Mrs. Thaine this morning that the death of Thaine was almost accidental. What I meant by that was this. When Miss Allwood and Brillhart met recently in London and planned this whole thing, with the object of getting their hands on to Mrs. Allwood's money, they decided that Brillhart should kill her, because he had no known connection with her and no apparent motive for her murder. But that, by itself, left Brillhart with no security at all that he would get any of her money. You can't put agreements of that sort down on paper, you can't go to law about them if they aren't honoured. And he didn't trust Miss Allwood to pay up when the time came. So he thought of a scheme that would put her in his power as much as he was going to be in hers. It was just the sort of scheme that would occur to a man whose fantasy runs to seeing himself doing dangerous missions behind the Japanese lines or in German-occupied Warsaw. A conspiratorial scheme. A scheme based on what's been done in the past by certain revolutionary groups who wanted to make sure of the absolute loyalty of their members. She also was to commit a murder. Just that. She was to commit a murder for no other reason than to make sure that she could never betray him. And she was to commit it wearing a red coat which would make her conspicuous, and she was to come back next day to make it even more certain that he could connect her with the crime if his own safety should require it."

"And Thaine was chosen at random?" Turkis said.

"Almost. But he was a man of size, an honest artist, and I think that's why Brillhart chose him as his victim. He hated him just because he was big and genuine. And for a little while there must have been a great joy for Brillhart in the belief that he could destroy Thaine safely and bring him down to a nothingness like himself."

"Nothingness?" Brillhart said in a vicious whisper. "How can you say that about me? What do you know of me, of my work, of what I might have been if I'd ever had the good fortune, the luck, the sheer luck, that always follows people like Thaine? He'd no more natural ability than I had, he just had luck and influence. But only for that one word, nothingness, I'm going to get my hands on you and——"

Turkis stepped forward. His hand fell on Brillhart's quivering shoulder.

"Much of this is by no means as clear to me as it appears to be to Mr. Emery," he said. "But I think you and I should have another talk, Mr. Brillhart."

XIX

It was raining again when Justin walked up the path to Grace's door. It was only light rain for the present, but darker clouds to the west threatened that it would soon grow heavier and continue perhaps for hours.

He found Grace lying on the sofa in her sitting-room, with cushions under her head. Her eyes were closed and she opened them only for an instant when Justin came in.

He sat down at the foot of the sofa.

"How are you?" he asked.

"I've the sort of headache that makes me feel I must have been mixing my drinks for a week," she said. "I don't like being arrested and I don't like being knocked out. From now on I'm against violence."

"You've heard everything, I suppose?"

"Yes, they're both under arrest, aren't they?"

"Yes."

"But has Turkis enough evidence to hold them? Will they be convicted?"

"I think so. For one thing, I think Brillhart will break down and incriminate the girl as much as he can, in the hope of making things easier for himself."

"The girl won't break down?"

"I don't know, but I think she's the less likely to do so. Just think of the bullet in the clock and what that probably meant."

"Wasn't it just bad shooting?"

"I don't think so. She put all the other shots where she wanted them. I think that bullet in the clock was a kind of bravado. When she saw that room full of clocks, all telling different times, she thought it would be a good joke to put a bullet into one of them. She'd probably read of how the time of death has sometimes been decided in murder cases or accidents by the victim's watch being broken, and so deliberately, with malice aforethought, she put a bullet into the clock over the fireplace."

"You're quite right, the sort of person who'd do that wouldn't break down too easily," Grace said.

"It may have been in rather the same spirit," he went on, "or else with a slightly more rational desire to throw suspicion on someone else, that she picked up Ben Eagan's watch from the table and threw it down on the floor beside Thaine's body, where you found it and thought that it meant there had been a fight between Thaine and Eagan."

"And my clock here, which they found at Mrs. Allwood's feet—that was just more over-elaboration, to make it look as if her murder was connected with Thaine's."

"Yes, yet actually it helped me to see the truth about that, because in fact that clock couldn't mean anything whatever. It was quite obviously a plant."

Grace opened her eyes, but winced at the light and closed them again.

"And but for the accident of your coming to see me that day, I suppose they'd have got away with it," she said.

"I doubt it, somehow. What really destroyed them had nothing to do with me."

"What did betray them?"

"The rain, the sun and a dog."

"Putting it like that, you make it sound like fate."

"You see, Brillhart left for London before the rain started, so he couldn't know that the old man wouldn't be at his usual window but would see and note the actual time when Doris went into the studio. And the sun helped to check the time, And the dog put the finger on her."

"And now," Grace said, "what's going to happen to you?"

"To me?" he said, a little surprised. "Well, I'll go back to London."

"To-day?"

"I think so."

"But what about your real reason for coming here?"

"What do you suppose my real reason was?"

" Oh, but that was always perfectly clear. You wanted to find out what you could about Marion. And actually we've hardly talked about her at all. And even if we'd talked about her, there isn't much I'd have been able to tell you, because, as I told you, we don't see much of one another nowadays. But look——" She reached out and picked up a slip of paper from a table. " Here's her address."

He took the paper and sat looking at the few words pencilled on it. He did not try to argue with Grace any more on this subject. He noted that Marion's home was close to London and it occurred to him that probably she visited London quite often.

" Thanks," he said, " and what about you ? "

" Oh, the doctor says I'm quite all right. This head doesn't mean anything."

" I meant, what about your life here ? Aren't you going to be—rather lonely ? "

" Well, the children will be home for the Christmas holidays soon."

" But Grace——"

She put out a hand to stop him.

" Don't," she said. " Don't argue with me. I'll get over it. I mean, I'll get over Ben. Really I want him to marry Hester—I think they'll fit one another and be quite happy. But I'm very glad they're going away from here."

" Why don't you come up to London for a while now, until the children come home ? "

" No, I'll stay. And don't worry about me, Justin. I'll get over it all, sooner or later."

" But——"

" No. And listen to me. What you must do is go and see Marion and find out if you really have got over her. Running away like you did, you'll never be quite sure till you've seen her. Personally, I don't believe you ever got over her at all, and I think you ought to face it."

He fingered the piece of paper she had given him. She had always had too much strength of will for him to be able to argue with her without to some extent losing his temper, and that, at the moment, would have been more than either of them could have borne. He put the slip of paper away in a pocket.

"Perhaps you're right," he said.

"And you must come here again sometime," she said, suddenly speaking in a hurried and not quite sincere tone of voice. "Only next time you might give me a little more warning, then I'll try to arrange things better. And don't wait another six years."

THE END